The Abbey Mysteries

The Silent Man

Other books in the series

The Buried Cross
The Scarlet Spring
The Drowned Sword

The Abbey Mysteries
The Silent Man

Cherith Baldry

OXFORD
UNIVERSITY PRESS

OXFORD

UNIVERSITY PRESS

Great Clarendon Street, Oxford OX2 6DP

Oxford University Press is a department of the University of Oxford.
It furthers the University's objective of excellence in research,
scholarship, and education by publishing worldwide in

Oxford New York

Auckland Bangkok Buenos Aires Cape Town
Chennai Dar es Salaam Delhi Hong Kong Istanbul Karachi
Kolkata Kuala Lumpur Madrid Melbourne Mexico City Mumbai
Nairobi São Paulo Shanghai Taipei Tokyo Toronto

Oxford is a registered trade mark of Oxford University Press
in the UK and in certain other countries

British Library Cataloguing in Publication Data available

ISBN 0 19 275363 0

1 3 5 7 9 10 8 6 4 2

Printed in Great Britain by
Cox & Wyman Ltd, Reading, Berkshire

Cast of Characters

In the village:

Geoffrey Mason, innkeeper of the Crown in Glastonbury

Idony, his wife

Gwyneth, their daughter

Hereward, their son

Owen Mason, Geoffrey's brother, a stonemason at work on the Abbey

Anne, his wife

Matt Green, a stonemason

Bedwyn, a workman

Finn Thorson, the local sheriff

Hawisa, his wife

Ivo and Amabel, their twin children, friends of Gwyneth and Hereward

Rhys Freeman, the local shopkeeper

Tom Smith, the local smith

Mari, his wife

Hywel, his brother

Dickon Carver, the local carpenter

Margery, his wife
Mistress Flax, a weaver
Wat and Hankin, brothers, servants at the Crown

At the Abbey:
Henry de Sully, Abbot of Glastonbury Abbey
Brother Barnabas, the abbey steward
Brother Padraig, the abbey infirmarian
Brother Milo, the abbey refectioner
Brother Simeon, his assistant, a novice monk
Brother Timothy, a young monk
Ralph FitzStephen, the king's steward, overseer of
the rebuilding of the abbey
Eleanor, his daughter
Hilde, Eleanor's nursemaid

Visitors to Glastonbury:
Godfrey de Massard, a priest from Wells Cathedral
Marion le Fevre, an embroideress, come to work
on the abbey's vestments
Ursus, a hermit living on Glastonbury Tor
Lord Robert Hardwycke, lord of a manor near
Wells
Edmund Hardwycke, his son

At Hardwycke:
Edmund's nursemaid
Martin, a servant
A guard

Glastonbury, south-west England,
AD 1190

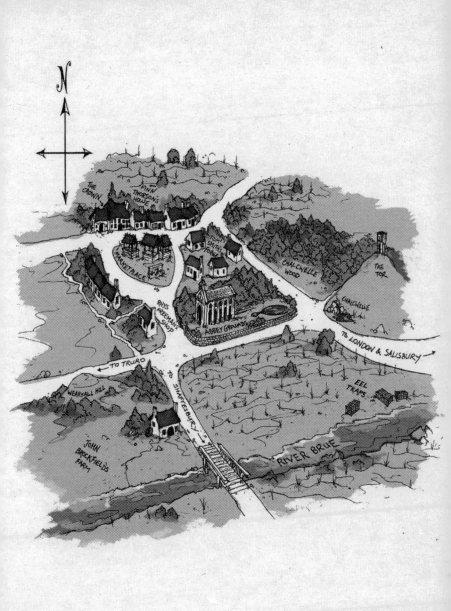

Chapter One

Fallen leaves crunched under Gwyneth Mason's feet as she hurried beside the half-built wall of Glastonbury Abbey. As she passed the gap where carts loaded with building materials could enter the abbey precinct, a sudden volley of sound— the strike of hammers against stone—told her the stonemasons were hard at work on the new church.

Gwyneth had no time to stop and see if her uncle Owen, who was one of the most important masons, was among the workmen. Her mother had sent her to buy salt, and she would be waiting for it in the kitchen of the Crown Inn so that she could cook the evening meal. Gwyneth could hardly believe that not long ago her father had been afraid he would have to close the inn. Since the disastrous fire at the abbey, few pilgrims had come to Glastonbury and the whole town had been sinking into poverty. For a while, work on the new abbey church had almost stopped, because there was no money to buy stone.

But now, less than a month after Gwyneth and her brother Hereward had recovered the bones of King Arthur and Queen Guinevere, pilgrims were beginning to return to the abbey. Everyone at the inn was run off their feet, and sometimes Gwyneth was tempted to wish that the famous bones had stayed buried.

The pilgrims who came to see the remains of the great king and his queen had money to spend in the village, and their contributions meant that Abbot Henry could pay for building materials again. As if echoing her thoughts, Gwyneth heard the creaking of wheels and saw a pair of straining mules pull a heavily-laden cart up the road from the landing-stage on the river where barges delivered the stone. Uncle Owen was leading the mules, while behind the cart walked a huge man Gwyneth had never seen before. His head was bowed so that his long black hair hid his face, but he was still several handspans taller than Owen Mason. His coarse woollen tunic was stretched tightly across his massive shoulders, and he seemed to cover the distance between the river and the abbey in just a few strides.

A shout from her brother roused Gwyneth from her curiosity. Hereward had already reached Rhys Freeman's shop, a few yards further down the street, and was waiting for her outside. Gwyneth picked up her skirt and hurried across the muddy cobbles to join him.

'Come on,' said Hereward, leading the way into the shop. 'Mother will be wondering where we've got to.'

Gwyneth followed him inside. Rhys Freeman was standing by a trestle table half-filled with earthenware pots, some with lids and others open, their contents hidden in shadow. He gave Hereward and Gwyneth a sullen look as they entered. The shopkeeper had never been friendly, but he disliked them even more since they had discovered that he was the thief who had taken Arthur's bones from the abbey.

The local sheriff, Finn Thorson, was there as well, examining a pile of reed baskets. Master Thorson straightened up as Gwyneth and Hereward came in, his head of wild red hair almost brushing the roofbeams. 'No pieces of the True Cross today, Master Freeman?' he asked, giving the children a wink. 'No saints' bones?'

Gwyneth tried not to laugh. She would never

forget the day when she and Hereward had broken into Rhys Freeman's cellar to find it stuffed full of fake holy relics, which the shop-keeper was selling for a good profit. That was why he had stolen Arthur's bones, so that he could sell fakes and pretend they were the real ones.

Master Freeman had lost a lot of his self-confident bluster after he had been punished for his crimes with a spell in the stocks. His grubby clothes seemed to hang on him as if he had lost weight. His shop looked dirty, too, and there were fewer goods on offer. Gwyneth was sure that he must be feeling the loss of his assistant, Osbert Teller, who had done all the cleaning and tidying. Osbert had fled from the village when his master's crimes were discovered.

Rhys Freeman shuffled his feet and looked down at a hole in his boot where his toenail was poking through. 'I've naught to do with that trade any more,' he protested. 'As you well know, Master Thorson.'

'Well, mind you keep it that way,' Finn Thorson said. 'I'm watching you, Rhys.' He left the shop, ducking his head to pass under the lintel of the door.

'And what do you want?' Rhys Freeman demanded rudely, turning to Gwyneth and Hereward. 'State your business and then be off with you.'

'Mother sent us for some salt, Master Freeman,' Gwyneth said, holding out a leather bag.

'And she said to tell you not to mix sand in with it this time,' Hereward added.

Master Freeman gave a bad-tempered snort as he snatched the bag from Gwyneth. 'Nobody has ever bought sand in my shop,' he muttered unconvincingly. Stamping over to a corner of the room, he scooped up a handful of salt from a barrel and thrust the full bag back at Gwyneth.

She licked her finger and tasted a little. It was definitely salt. 'Thank you, Master Freeman,' she said, bobbing a curtsy. 'Will you mark it up to the Crown? Mother says—'

A crash sounded from the street, followed by shouting. Hereward darted across to the doorway and looked out. 'Come and see!' he called. 'Uncle Owen's cart has broken a wheel.' He hurried outside.

Gwyneth said a hasty farewell to Rhys Freeman and followed her brother. A small crowd was already gathering, drawn by the noise like moths to a candle flame. It looked as if a front wheel had given way just as the cart approached the gap in the abbey wall, tipping it onto its side. Splinters of wood were scattered around and the huge block of stone the cart had been carrying had slid to the ground. The pair of mules had scrambled up and were braying in distress, lashing out with their hooves as they tried to free themselves from the twisted ropes.

Hereward was already running across the street to soothe the terrified animals. As Gwyneth watched, her uncle drew a knife from his belt and slashed through the mules' harness. She paused to fasten the thongs on the bag of salt, then hurried after her brother, dodging through the curious villagers until she reached the cart. Two or three more stonemasons were standing around, surveying the damage with disgusted expressions. The tall man that Gwyneth had seen following the cart was struggling to lift the stone. She could see the strain in his shoulder muscles and in the lines that stood out on his face.

'Steady!' one of the masons shouted, as the cart lurched and the stone shifted.

The man made no response, but gripped the stone even tighter.

Matt Green slapped him on the back. 'Give over, man! We'll need ropes and mules to shift that.'

The man jerked upright, startled, and his hand struck against one of the snapped shafts of the cart. Blood seeped from his clenched fist, scarlet against the grey stone. Gwyneth gasped with sympathy when she saw a long splinter embedded deep in the ball of his thumb, but the man himself made no sound.

'Bedwyn?' The voice was Owen Mason's; he stepped up quickly and took the man's hand in his own to examine the injury. 'That needs cleaning. Better take it to Brother Padraig and have it seen to right away.'

The man shook his head, but Owen's voice grew more forceful. 'Don't be a fool. What if the wound turns bad? Here, Gwyneth—'Owen's gaze lighted on his niece— 'go with Bedwyn into the abbey and make sure he sees Brother Padraig.' Drawing closer, he added quietly, 'Bedwyn hasn't worked for us long, and up to now he's been down at the landing-stage where we unload the stone, so he doesn't know the

monks. You'll need to explain what happened;
the man never speaks.'

Gwyneth opened her eyes very wide. 'Yes,
uncle,' she said at once.

'Thank you, Gwyneth,' said her uncle. His
mouth curved in a smile and he whispered,
'There's no need to be afeared of Bedwyn. Even
though he doesn't speak, he can understand you,
and he'd not hurt a fly.'

A little nervously, Gwyneth reached out and
touched Bedwyn's sleeve. 'If you'll come with
me, master . . .'

Bedwyn turned to look down at her. His face
was harsh and weathered, surrounded by a tangle
of dark hair. For a moment Gwyneth felt a tremor
of concern, until she saw that his deep-set eyes
v.ere gentle and shy, like a startled deer.

She found herself smiling up at the huge man.
To her surprise he bowed his head to her, his
uninjured hand on his chest; it was a strange,
courtly gesture that made Gwyneth feel she
should be curtsying to him. Instead, she beckoned him to follow her down the street towards
the main gate of the abbey. Hereward handed
over the quietened mules to Matt Green, and
fell in beside them.

The crowd separated to let them pass without a sound. Gwyneth noticed that some of the villagers glanced warily at Bedwyn, and Tom Smith's wife Mari drew her little boy closer to her skirt. Gwyneth felt a sting of indignation on behalf of the stonemason who followed her steadily, a few paces behind.

The door of the Lady Chapel was open when Gwyneth and Hereward led Bedwyn under the archway of the abbey gate. The monks were filing out from the service of nones into the pale autumn sunlight. Gwyneth spotted the tall figure of Abbot Henry, closely followed by Father Godfrey de Massard, who was visiting Glastonbury Abbey from the cathedral at Wells. Everyone in the village knew that Dean Alexander of Wells wanted to bring Glastonbury under his authority. Gwyneth and Hereward were convinced that Father Godfrey was spying for the dean, gleefully telling him when things went wrong in the village. The more the abbey struggled to rebuild itself after the fire, the sooner Dean Alexander would be able to take it over.

Just then, Brother Padraig appeared from the chapel, and Gwyneth forgot about Father Godfrey as she hurried towards him. 'Brother

11

Padraig!' she exclaimed. 'This is Bedwyn, one of the stonemasons. His hand is hurt, look!'

'Peace, Gwyneth.' The abbey infirmarian rested his hand on her arm for a moment. 'All will be well, with God's good help.' He turned to the stonemason and held out his hands so that Bedwyn could put his injured one into them.

Blood was still welling from the gash and Brother Padraig hissed softly through his teeth as he examined it. Gwyneth watched anxiously, waiting for the monk's verdict. Brother Padraig was an experienced healer, skilled with herbs and poultices, but a stonemason's hands were the most important tools of his trade.

'A nasty cut,' he said at last. 'Come with me to the infirmary. I'll bathe it and bind on a poultice of comfrey root, and please God it will give you no more trouble.'

He turned away, motioning to Bedwyn to follow him, and then halted, staring towards the abbey gateway. Gwyneth followed his gaze and her eyes widened as she saw the procession that was making its way through the gates.

At the front was a tall man riding a magnificent chestnut horse. He wore a blue cloak lined with ermine, fastened on one shoulder with a gold clasp and thrown back to reveal an embroidered velvet tunic. He reined in his horse before he reached the chapel and looked around.

Behind him came half a dozen men-at-arms wearing chain mail covered by scarlet surcoats. They were riding on either side of a litter slung between two horses. Its four-poster framework was made of carved and gilded wood, like a gigantic bed, but instead of embroidered bed-hangings the closed curtains were of deerskin. At the very end of the procession was a heavily loaded cart, drawn by a mule and driven by yet another man-at-arms.

'More pilgrims?' Hereward murmured into Gwyneth's ear. 'Rich ones, by the look of it!'

Gwyneth nodded. A lord such as this could pay for the rebuilding of the whole nave. She guessed that his lady was being carried in the litter, being too delicate to endure a long ride on horseback.

Brother Barnabas, the abbey steward, appeared from the gatehouse and hurried towards the nobleman, who dismounted and tossed his reins to the nearest man-at-arms. Gwyneth saw that he was older than she had thought at first and his handsome face looked tired and strained.

Brother Barnabas began to welcome the newcomers, but the nobleman interrupted his courteous greeting.

'Enough of that.' His tone showed that he was used to being obeyed. 'I have an urgent errand to one of your monks. Take me at once to Brother Padraig.'

Gwyneth glanced at the infirmarian, catching a look of surprise on his face. He nodded to Bedwyn, murmured, 'One moment,' and set off across the grass towards the nobleman and his retinue. Gwyneth and Hereward followed him curiously.

As they approached, Gwyneth saw a thin white hand grasp the edge of one of the deerskin curtains on the litter and draw it back. To her astonishment, instead of the fine lady she had imagined, she found she was looking into the pale, scared face of a young boy.

Chapter Two

'I am Lord Robert Hardwycke,' the nobleman introduced himself to Brother Barnabas, slipping his hands out of scarlet leather gloves. 'My estates lie beyond Wells, and I've come to consult your infirmarian on a matter of most grave urgency.'

'I am Brother Padraig,' said the infirmarian, stepping forward. 'How may I serve you, sir?'

Lord Robert Hardwycke gestured towards the litter. 'I have brought my only son, Edmund. He is eight years old and suffers from the falling sickness. I will give rich gifts to the abbey if you can cure him.'

'No need to speak of gifts,' Brother Padraig replied mildly. 'I'll be glad to use what skills God has given me. If it pleases you, my lord, go with Brother Barnabas, who will show you to our guest lodgings. I will come shortly and examine your son there.'

Lord Robert frowned. 'You will not come with us now?'

Brother Padraig glanced back to where Bedwyn was still waiting. 'Your pardon, my lord. This man's hand is injured. I must take him to the infirmary to bind it.'

Lord Robert raised his eyebrows in displeasure. 'My son's need is urgent,' he protested.

'And a workman has no greater need than his hands,' Brother Padraig answered firmly. 'Do not fear, my lord, I will be with you before you are well settled in your lodgings.'

He turned away with a courteous bow, bringing the argument to a close. As he did so, Gwyneth noticed something fall out of the litter from underneath the deerskin curtains.

Hereward had seen it too and darted across the grass. Gwyneth joined him beside the litter as he picked up the object—a beautifully carved and painted model of a horse—and held it out. 'I think you dropped this?'

The little boy's face appeared again and he reached out to take the horse. Thin white fingers curled around it. 'Thank you.' His voice was scarcely more than a whisper. 'Is this Glastonbury Abbey?' he asked, drawing back the curtain

16

further and gazing round the precinct with huge eyes.

'That's right,' said Hereward.

The boy sank back against the heaped cushions of the litter, his lashes fluttering as if he was about to drift into sleep. 'It's not like I imagined . . .' he murmured. 'It looks only half-built.'

'But the new church will be more splendid than anything else,' Gwyneth said encouragingly. 'Did you know the monks found King Arthur's grave not long ago?'

Edmund Hardwycke looked up with a flicker of interest in his eyes. 'I heard about that. Is it really true?'

'Yes, really,' Hereward assured him. 'We saw his coffin dug up. King Arthur's bones were in it, and Queen Guinevere's. They're in the chapel—we'll show you. Do you want to come now?'

For a moment Edmund looked eager, but then his excitement faded and he sank back again on the cushions. 'Not now,' he replied. 'I'm not well enough. Father will say I must rest after the journey.'

Gwyneth thought he had been resting already in the litter, but she said nothing. Edmund certainly looked frail and ill, his breath coming in shallow gasps as if even talking for such a little while had exhausted him.

'Do you like tales of King Arthur?' she asked.

Edmund nodded. 'Father Paul gives me my lessons, but if I'm too tired he reads to me out of a great book of father's, tales of King Arthur and his knights, and the evil witch Morgan le Fay. I wish I—'

His father's voice interrupted him. 'Edmund, draw back the curtain. Do you want to catch a chill?'

Gwyneth turned around to see Lord Robert Hardwycke standing over her. His expression was disapproving, but there was genuine anxiety in his eyes as he looked down at his son.

'Yes, father,' Edmund said obediently. 'Goodbye,' he added with a glance at Gwyneth and Hereward, before he pulled the curtains closed again.

'We'll try to come and see you again,' Hereward promised.

Lord Robert snapped an order to his men, who began to steer the litter in the direction of the guest lodgings behind Brother Barnabas. As the men moved away, the nobleman hesitated for a moment. 'You must understand that my son is ill,' he said to Gwyneth and Hereward. 'He cannot run and play as other children do.'

Gwyneth's throat felt tight with pity. 'We understand, my lord,' she said. 'But with your leave we'll come and spend some time with him. He might get lonely, being so far away from home.'

Lord Robert looked blank, as if he didn't know how to answer.

'We're Hereward and Gwyneth Mason, from the Crown Inn,' Hereward added. 'The holy brothers here know us.'

Lord Robert gave a curt nod. 'Very well. You have my leave to visit him.' Without waiting for a reply he turned and hurried after the departing litter.

Hereward watched the procession make its way slowly towards the guest lodgings. Then he turned to Gwyneth. 'Mother mentioned that there were no cloves in the market this morning. Since we're here, I'll go to the kitchen and ask the monks if they can spare any.'

Gwyneth nodded. 'Very well. I'll see you back at home. And watch out for Brother Milo!' she

19

teased. The refectioner in charge of the kitchen was famous for his short temper.

Hereward pulled a face and trudged across the precinct, following the scent of roasting meat and fragrant spices. The abbey kitchen was a long, low-ceilinged room, a haven of warmth on a chilly autumn day. Bunches of herbs and onions hung from the beams, while wooden shelves fixed to the white-washed walls held an array of iron pots and pans. Halfway down one wall a fire burnt brightly in a cavernous fireplace where one or two pots were simmering.

Hereward paused in the doorway and looked round for Brother Milo, but the abbey refectioner was nowhere to be seen today. He breathed a sigh of relief.

A couple of monks whom he did not know were standing by one of the long tables, chopping onions. At the far end of the kitchen he recognized Brother Simeon, a young novice who had yet to take his final vows, standing on a stool with the sleeves of his habit rolled up to bend over the huge iron cauldron that the abbey used as a fish tank. A pattern shaped like a bird was etched into one of the huge curved panels that made up the sides.

As Hereward drew closer, the novice hauled out a gleaming silver fish, both hands clasped round it just below its head.

'Brother Simeon!' Hereward said.

The novice jumped and the fish slithered out of his grasp and flopped back into the tank, showering Brother Simeon with water. He grabbed the top of the cauldron to stop himself falling off the stool. 'Hereward!' he exclaimed. 'Don't sneak up on me like that!'

'I'm sorry,' said Hereward. 'Mother sent me to ask Brother Milo to lend her some cloves.'

Brother Simeon sighed and stepped down. 'Of course. I'm sure Brother Milo would be glad to help.' He cast a glance back at the fish tank. 'That was the abbot's dinner that just escaped. It took me ages to catch it.'

'I'm sorry,' Hereward repeated.

Brother Simeon went to a shelf where some earthenware jars were standing, and returned a moment later with a handful of cloves tied up in a scrap of linen. 'Here you are. Now get out of here and let me catch that fish again before Brother Milo comes back.'

Hereward thanked him and escaped, tucking the cloves into his pouch. His mother would be well pleased with the extra spices for their guests' evening meal, and, in spite of the accident with the cart, he would be back in time to help Wat and Hankin bed down the visitors' horses for the night.

'And you should have seen Lord Robert's clothes!' Gwyneth said. 'His cloak lined with fur, and his velvet tunic, with beautiful gold embroidery . . . but not as good as yours,' she added loyally.

Marion le Fevre smiled as she looked round from her embroidery frame, her needle poised in slender fingers. 'He must indeed be a wealthy man. I shall be sorry not to see his wonderful clothes for myself. You know very well that I will never set foot in the abbey grounds.'

Gwyneth nodded. The beautiful embroideress had come to Glastonbury to work on vestments and altar cloths for the new church, but the thought of the damage caused by the fire upset her so much that she refused to enter the precinct. Not even news of the fine new Lady Chapel, or the church rising so majestically from the rubble and ashes, would make her change her mind.

The first of the altar cloths was on the embroidery frame now, set close to the window of the best bedchamber in the Crown. On a background of white silk, Marion was embroidering lilies in a rainbow of coloured threads. Gwyneth had never seen such exquisite work.

It was the morning after Lord Robert Hardwycke's arrival at the abbey, and she had taken the first chance she could to share the news with Marion. 'Mother says there's no better healer anywhere than Brother Padraig,' she added as she watched the embroideress's needle flashing in and out.

'There's something I must ask your mother,' Marion le Fevre said after she had stitched in silence for a few moments and Gwyneth had busied herself winding green silk onto a bobbin. 'Is there a woman in the village who would come and help me with my work? I need someone to set up another frame, and trace patterns onto the silk—perhaps even do a little of the background stitching.'

'Yes, I'm sure mother will know someone,' Gwyneth replied. An idea came to her and she added, 'You might ask my aunt Anne. She's a good seamstress. She made me this gown.' She spread her blue-grey skirt so that Marion could see.

'Would she come, do you think?'

'I expect so, mistress. Uncle Owen is at work all day at the abbey, and they have no children, so she might be glad of the company.'

A sharp rap on the door interrupted them and Hereward's voice came from outside. 'Mistress le Fevre?'

'Come in,' Marion called.

Hereward stepped inside the room, ducking his head respectfully. 'Lord Ralph FitzStephen is here, mistress. He wants to see how your work proceeds.'

'Of course,' said Marion, smiling. 'Tell him to come up.'

Hereward disappeared again, and Marion examined her work, letting her fingers trail over the embroidered silk. 'Do you think my efforts will please Lord Ralph?' she asked.

'I'm sure they will!' said Gwyneth.

Lord Ralph FitzStephen was the king's steward, sent to Glastonbury to supervise the rebuilding of the abbey. Gwyneth could not help being a bit nervous of him, because he had a quick temper and a scathing tongue. But today

24

the royal steward seemed to be in a genial mood. Gwyneth was surprised to see that he held his little daughter Eleanor by the hand; she was a slender, delicate-featured girl with long golden curls and huge blue eyes, not at all like her dark, hawk-faced father.

'Good morrow, Mistress le Fevre,' said Lord Ralph. 'I hope you don't mind that I've brought my daughter to visit you? It's lonely for her at the abbey, with only a nursemaid to care for her.'

Gwyneth and Hereward exchanged a glance. Their father had told them that the little girl's mother had died of a fever six years ago, when Eleanor was only a baby. Gwyneth couldn't imagine what it would be like never to know a mother's care, but anyone who saw Lord Ralph and his daughter together could see that Eleanor meant the world to her father.

The child shyly drew close to Lord Ralph as he led her into the room.

Marion le Fevre rose from her chair and sank into a deep curtsy. 'It is kind of you to come, my lord. Hereward, fetch wine for Lord Ralph, and some of your mother's spiced cakes.'

'No need.' Lord Ralph gestured to Hereward, halting him before he could obey the order. 'We can't stay. I wanted to make sure that the work is going well, and ask if you need anything.' He gave one of his rare smiles. 'Besides, I thought Eleanor would like to see the lovely things you're making.'

'But of course!' Marion le Fevre held out her hands to the little girl. 'Come, child.'

Eleanor hung back, but when her father gave her a gentle push she crossed the room to stand in front of the embroidery frame.

'What a beautiful child!' Marion exclaimed. 'Such hair—like spun gold!' She lifted a long curl and ran it through her fingers.

The little girl pulled away and ran back to her father to bury her head in his cloak.

Lord Ralph looked vexed. 'Now, Eleanor, there's nothing to be afraid of,' he chided. 'Mistress le Fevre, I'm sorry—'

'No need to ask pardon,' Marion le Fevre replied, her green eyes shining up at the steward. 'She will come to know me better in time, I hope. Lord Ralph, won't you come and see if you approve of my work?'

Lord Ralph left his daughter by the door while he went to admire Mistress le Fevre's embroidery. Gwyneth held out her hand to Eleanor. 'Come and sit with me,' she invited. 'You remember us, don't you? We've met before at the abbey. Would you like to help me with the thread?'

Eleanor nodded and came over to kneel on the floor beside Gwyneth. 'There's a new boy at the abbey,' she confided shyly after a moment, not lifting her eyes from the skein of thread she was spooling.

'Is that Edmund Hardwycke?' said Hereward, crossing the room to sit on the end of the chest where Marion stored her fabrics.

Eleanor looked up and nodded. 'Father says I have to be quiet, because Edmund can't run and play like me. So I showed him my doll Melusine, and I took my new kitten to see him.' Her blue eyes danced. 'She climbed all the way up his bed curtains, and made him laugh.'

'That was kind, Eleanor,' said Gwyneth. She remembered the solemn little face behind the deerskin curtain. 'I don't think Edmund laughs very much.'

'If we've time, we'll visit him later on today,' said Hereward.

'Come and see me too,' said Eleanor. 'Then I can show you my kitten.'

'So long as you don't make too much noise

and tire Edmund,' Lord Ralph said; he had turned away from Marion le Fevre in time to catch the last few words of the conversation. 'Three great strong creatures like you—yes, even you, my lady Eleanor.' He ruffled his daughter's hair and she giggled.

'Is Edmund very ill?' Gwyneth asked.

Lord Ralph nodded, looking more sombre. 'I fear so. Brother Padraig examined him yesterday, and again this morning. From the little that he said, I fear there is nothing he can do for the boy.'

'But you don't mean . . . you're not saying Edmund might die?' Hereward exclaimed, his eyes wide with shock.

Gwyneth held her breath while she waited for Lord Ralph's answer. Edmund had not fussed or complained about his illness in the brief time she spent with him—just long enough to learn that he loved the tales of Arthur as much as she did. She could not bear to think that he might die.

'I cannot say,' Lord Ralph replied at last. He glanced uneasily at Eleanor, as if he did not want to discuss death in front of his daughter. 'He is in God's hands.'

'I shall pray for the poor child.' Marion le Fevre spoke from her seat by the embroidery frame. 'It's the least I can do.'

Gwyneth gripped the bobbin so hard that it dug painfully into her hand. The embroideress's eyes were brimming with tears. How sensitive she was, to be so upset over a boy she had never seen!

Then Marion blinked her tears away. 'Though I can do nothing for Edmund,' she said to Lord Ralph, 'I can do something for you, Eleanor. My dear, would you like me to make you a special embroidered gown?'

Eleanor nodded shyly.

'Mistress, that's expecting too much,' Lord Ralph protested. 'I can't ask it of you, as well as all the work you have to do for the abbey.'

'But you are not asking,' Marion le Fevre pointed out with a dazzling smile. 'And my work for the abbey will not be neglected, I assure you. Please, Lord Ralph, it would give me great pleasure to sew for such a lovely child.'

'Well, if you're sure, then we'd be happy to accept,' said Lord Ralph. 'Eleanor, say thank you to Mistress le Fevre.'

Eleanor bobbed a little curtsy. 'Thank you.'

'I shall buy some material and set to work right away,' Marion promised.

Thanking her again, Lord Ralph took his leave. Hereward escorted him and Eleanor downstairs, while Gwyneth tidied up the embroidery silks.

'I must go,' she said to Marion, who had bent her head over her stitching again. 'Mother will expect me to help with the mid-day meal.'

Marion turned her head and smiled at her. 'Of course. And don't forget to ask about a helper for me.'

'I won't, I promise.'

When Gwyneth reached the foot of the stairs, Hereward was just returning from saying goodbye to Marion le Fevre's guests.

'Hereward, do you think Brother Padraig will have any idea what to do for Edmund?' she asked. 'I've never heard that any of the monks suffered from the falling sickness.'

'Or anyone in the village,' Hereward agreed. 'But we might be able to help,' he went on. 'Why don't we find Ursus and ask him? Remember how he healed my ankle?'

Gwyneth remembered very well. She would never forget their first encounter with the mysterious hermit who lived on the slopes of

Glastonbury Tor. Hereward had hurt his ankle falling into an eel trap, and Ursus had bound it up with herbs which had healed it so quickly that within a day or two there was not even a scar to be seen.

'Of course!' she said. 'Ursus will know what to do. We'll go and look for him straight after dinner.'

'Mother, we want to go and look for Ursus this afternoon,' said Gwyneth, scrubbing vigorously at an iron pot. The mid-day meal was over and she was in the kitchen, helping Idony Mason to clear up.

Idony glanced round as she wiped her hands on a cloth. 'Well, we're nearly done here,' she said, smiling. 'You've worked hard.'

'Then we can? We need to find Ursus to see if he knows any cure for the falling sickness.'

'Oh, for that poor little mite at the abbey,' said her mother. 'Yes, of course you can go, but don't stay out too late.'

Gwyneth rinsed out the pot, dried her hands, and fetched her cloak from where it hung on the back of the kitchen door. Stepping out into the

31

inn yard, she spotted Hereward tossing a handful of corn to the chickens.

'Are you ready?' she called to him.

'Just finishing,' Hereward replied. He shook the last grains of corn out of the bag and darted off to return the bag to the storeroom while Gwyneth waited.

They set out, taking the road out of the village past Tom Smith's forge. An icy wind was blowing and the market traders were shivering at their stalls, wrapped in cloaks and hoods and blowing on their fingers to keep warm. The villagers and pilgrims hurried over their bargaining, as if they wanted to get out of the cold as quickly as they could.

Leaving the village behind, Gwyneth and Hereward followed a path that wound through hazel bushes towards Glastonbury Tor. The ground grew wetter as they approached the river that ran round the bottom of the Tor; the wind made a rattling sound in the tops of the dry reeds, and piping calls came from unseen birds. Gwyneth shivered. Here in the marshes, with the top half of the Tor veiled in autumnal mist, it was easy to imagine that the legends were real. Were Arthur's bones all that was left of him, or was he waiting somewhere in the hills, as the old tales said, until it was his time to come again?

'I can't see Ursus.' Practical as always, Hereward's voice came from just behind her. 'Ursus! Where are you?'

His shout disturbed a couple of ducks that rose from the water with a noisy beating of wings and flapped away across the river. But there was no answer from the hermit.

Gwyneth sighed. 'It seems that he only turns up when we're not looking for him.'

'Well, he can't be expected to know that Edmund needs his help,' Hereward pointed out. 'Let's head for the Tor.'

Reaching the bank, they followed the river in the direction of the round, flat-topped hill, but there was still no sign of Ursus.

'I wish we knew where he lives,' Gwyneth said. 'Then we could find him easily. After all, the other hermits on the Tor have little huts, don't they?'

'That's true.' Hereward pushed back a branch that was hanging over the narrow path. 'But if he wanted us to know, he would have shown us.'

They went on searching until the short day drew to its end and the light began to fade.

'We'd better go back,' Gwyneth said. She had no wish to be wandering through the marshes after dark, with no lantern to guide them back to the safety of the road.

'Ursus! Can you hear us?' Hereward tried shouting once more, but the only reply was the rustle of some unseen creature in the reeds.

Admitting defeat, Gwyneth turned and began to lead the way back to the village. 'We'll try again tomorrow,' she said.

'Why don't we visit Edmund on the way home?' Hereward suggested. Jumping up, he grabbed a late cluster of hazelnuts from one of the bushes and thrust them into his pouch. 'He might enjoy these. I don't suppose he's ever gathered them for himself,' he added sombrely.

Night had fallen by the time they reached the abbey. Lights showed in the windows of the guest lodgings, a low building of grey stone to the left of the gatehouse.

When Gwyneth and Hereward pushed open the outer door, they almost collided with a young monk on his way out. It was Brother Timothy, the son of the village potter, who had been a friend of theirs before he took holy orders. As she greeted him, Gwyneth noticed a grave look on his bony face, quite different from his usual cheerful air. 'Is anything the matter?' she asked.

Brother Timothy nodded. 'It's young Edmund Hardwycke. His father brought him to vespers in the chapel, and the poor lad fell down in a fit. Brother Padraig is putting him to bed.'

'Is it all right to visit him?' Hereward asked.

'You can go in and see,' Brother Timothy replied, pointing to a door a few paces further along the passage. 'But if Brother Padraig or Lord Robert send you away, then you must leave at once.'

'Yes, of course,' said Gwyneth.

'I shall go and pray for the boy's recovery,' said Brother Timothy as he hurried out.

They went up to the door Brother Timothy had shown them. When Gwyneth knocked, Lord Robert's voice called, 'Come in!'

The room was brightly lit with firelight and candles. Edmund lay in bed against one wall, with Brother Padraig bending over him. The bed's coverings and hangings were made from heavy brocade and fur, far richer than anything the monks would have provided. Gwyneth wondered if Lord Robert had brought them himself, for the sake of his son's comfort.

Brother Padraig was raising Edmund with an arm around his shoulders, and holding a cup to his lips. Edmund's eyes were open, but his head drooped against Brother Padraig's arm as if it was too heavy for him to hold up. He took a sip of whatever the cup contained and turned his face away.

'Drink all of it, if you please, Master Edmund,' said Brother Padraig. 'It will do you good.'

The boy's father was restlessly pacing the room. He paid no attention to Gwyneth and Hereward until Hereward went over and bowed to him.

'We've come to visit Edmund, sir,' he said. 'We brought him some nuts. But we'll go if—'

'No, stay, stay.' Lord Robert halted in front of Hereward. His hair was ruffled, and his fine velvet tunic rumpled and laced crookedly. Lines of worry were etched in his face, and as he began pacing again his eyes kept straying to the bed where his son lay.

Gwyneth and Hereward retreated towards the fire, out of the way. Almost at once the door opened again to let in Eleanor FitzStephen and her nursemaid Hilde.

Under one arm Eleanor held Melusine, a fine French doll with flaxen hair and embroidered skirts. With the other hand she was trying to hang on to a small black kitten that had scrambled up onto her shoulder and was tangling its paws in her hair.

'Gwyneth! Hereward!' Eleanor cried, bouncing across the room. 'Look, I've brought Kitty to see Edmund!'

'Shhh,' Gwyneth whispered. 'We have to be quiet. Edmund was taken ill in the chapel.'

'There, Miss Eleanor,' said Hilde. The girl looked flustered, her brown hair beginning to escape from its braid. 'I said it was too late to be visiting Master Edmund.'

'Father said I could come,' Eleanor retorted, 'and besides, Kitty will make Edmund laugh.'

She sat on a stool Hilde placed for her, while Gwyneth and Hereward crouched down beside her to admire the kitten.

'She's a bad, scratchy little thing,' Eleanor said, giggling. Suddenly serious, she added, 'She wants Edmund to play with her.'

'He can't just now,' Gwyneth said gently. 'You know he isn't strong like you.'

'I know, but . . .' The little girl brightened again. 'Brother Padraig will make him better, and then he'll be able to play.'

Gwyneth wished she could believe it. Edmund had finished drinking and was lying very still and silent. When Brother Padraig straightened up from the bedside, his face was graver than Gwyneth had ever seen it.

'Well?' Lord Robert demanded, his voice raw with anxiety.

The infirmarian went to him, laid a hand on his arm, and drew him to the far side of the room. He spoke in a low voice, but Gwyneth heard what he said.

'Lord Robert, I have never seen such a bad case of falling sickness. I will try what remedies I have, but I am not sure how much I can do to help him.'

'There must be something you can do!'

Edmund and Eleanor both looked up, startled by Lord Robert's exclamation.

'You are welcome to stay here as long as you want, my lord,' Brother Padraig said calmly, 'and I will do my best for your son. For tonight, go to the kitchen and ask Brother Milo for a hot posset. At least that should give the boy a good night's rest. Tomorrow I will try what more I can do.'

Lord Robert stood with clenched hands, as if

he wanted to lash out at something. His face was working, but he managed to hang on to self-control. 'No, Brother,' he said at last. 'If you can hold out no more hope, then we will leave at first light. If my son is to die, he will do it in his own home, not here among strangers. His mother died giving birth to him,' he added, his voice choking. 'He is all I have.' He sank into the nearest chair and covered his face with his hands.

Gwyneth scooped up the kitten, ignoring its plaintive miaow, and carried it across the room to Edmund's bed, hoping to distract him from his father's distress.

Eleanor trotted after her, while Hereward pulled the hazelnuts out of his pouch and set them on the table beside Edmund's bed. 'You might enjoy those when you're feeling better,' he said. 'I'm Hereward, and that's my sister, Gwyneth. We met yesterday in the precinct, do you remember?'

'Yes, I remember. Thank you.' Edmund's voice was even more feeble than before but there was a spark of amusement in his eyes when he looked at the kitten.

Gwyneth glanced towards his father and away again, back to where Eleanor's kitten was romping happily on the bedcover. She felt they should not have been a witness to Lord Robert's grief.

'We *must* find Ursus,' she whispered to Hereward, who nodded.

With a massive effort, Lord Robert pulled himself to his feet and strode across the room to the bed where his son lay. 'We will go home tomorrow, Edmund.' Gwyneth was surprised at how gentle his voice had become. 'We will see again what our own physician can do.'

'Yes, father.' Edmund's eyes were shadowed as he stroked the kitten with one pale, wasted hand. 'But may I see Arthur's bones before we go?'

'Yes, of course,' Lord Robert replied, sounding surprised.

'I'll show you,' Eleanor chimed in. 'My father was there when they were dug up. He was one of the first people ever to see them.'

'That's a good girl.' Lord Robert rested his hand for a moment on Eleanor's golden hair, looking at the little girl's rosy cheeks and bright eyes. Gwyneth wondered if he was thinking how different she was from his own son. 'Come early, though, because we have a long journey ahead of us.'

His gaze fell on his son again, and Gwyneth's heart twisted with pain at the grief she could see in his face. Briefly she considered telling Lord Robert about the hermit who might be able to help, but she guessed that he would have no faith in a man whom scarcely anyone had seen.

She thought back to the empty marshes under the darkening winter sky. *Why wasn't Ursus there today?* she asked herself despairingly.

Chapter Three

Next morning dawned bright and cold, and Geoffrey Mason whistled cheerfully as he unloaded sacks of flour from a cart in the inn yard. Gwyneth walked under the archway to the street and listened to the buzz of noise and chatter from the market-place, which was much busier now that the rain had stopped.

'I'm sure you'll find some pretty material for Eleanor's gown,' she said to Marion le Fevre, who was walking beside her. 'There's so much more to buy now that the pilgrims are coming back again.'

The embroideress smiled. 'I hope you're right, Gwyneth. Words can't express how much I long for the abbey to be restored again.'

'It won't be long now.' Hereward was on Mistress le Fevre's other side, carrying Idony Mason's basket. 'The church walls are growing higher every day. If you would only come and see—'

'Oh, no, no, I couldn't possibly!' Marion le Fevre halted, one slender hand pressed to her cheek. 'Don't speak of it, Hereward.'

'Yes, you know how much it upsets her,' Gwyneth added, cross with her brother for forgetting.

Hereward flushed, and Marion reached out to touch his shoulder. 'Perhaps one day,' she said, with a forgiving smile, 'but not yet.'

They crossed the street towards the stalls clustered around the market cross. Gwyneth spotted Mistress Carver, the carpenter's wife, behind her stall piled high with wooden boxes, bowls, and cups. On the stall beside Mistress Carver's, Finn Thorson's wife Hawisa was bargaining for eggs with one of the farmers from outside the village.

Before Gwyneth could lead Mistress le Fevre towards the linen-weaver's stall, she heard the sound of horses and turned to see Lord Robert Hardwycke and his retinue emerge from the abbey gateway.

She was wondering whether she dared approach Lord Robert and ask how Edmund was, when the little boy's litter drew level with them and his hand appeared to pull back the deerskin curtains. His pale face peered out and he called, 'Gwyneth! Hereward!'

Hereward darted across to him at once. Gwyneth hesitated, glancing at Marion.

'Go and speak to your friend,' said the embroideress. 'You'll find me at Mistress Flax's linen stall.'

With a word of thanks Gwyneth dashed off. When she reached the litter she heard Edmund say in his rasping whisper, 'I saw Arthur's bones! They looked . . . strange.' He drew his fur coverings closer as if he felt the cold.

'According to the old stories, King Arthur is sleeping under the Tor,' Gwyneth told him proudly. 'And one day he'll come again.'

'But not everyone believes that,' Hereward added.

'I do,' Edmund insisted. His eyes were very bright. 'I should like to be a knight, and ride into battle with my king.' His excitement faded and his voice was unsteady as he finished, 'But I never will.'

'Perhaps one day you'll get better . . .' Gwyneth tried hard to find words to encourage him.

Edmund shrugged. 'Perhaps.'

A shout came from the head of the procession.

'Edmund, hurry up and say farewell,' his father called. 'It's bad for you to be out in the cold air.'

Edmund lay back on his cushions. 'I must go,' he said. 'Goodbye.'

He let the curtain fall and the litter moved off, swaying between the mules that carried it. The rest of the procession followed with the laden cart at the rear, flanked by a couple of men-at-arms.

Gwyneth watched them depart down the street and turn the corner on to the road that led to Wells. 'I wish we'd managed to find Ursus,' she sighed.

'We still can.' Hereward had a familiar determined glint in his eye. 'He'll know what herbs to use, and we'll get them to Edmund somehow.'

Gwyneth immediately felt more cheerful. She knew Hereward was right. The hermit Ursus always appeared when they needed him most. Remembering his tanned face and smiling blue eyes, she trusted him not to fail them now.

Returning to the market, Hereward went to buy spices and honey for their mother, while Gwyneth found Marion le Fevre standing in front of Mistress Flax's stall. It was the most eye-catching of all, draped with lengths of linen in different colours.

The embroideress was holding up a piece of blue material. 'Look!' she exclaimed as soon as she saw Gwyneth. 'Have you ever seen such fine quality? Mistress Flax is so skilful!'

The plump linen weaver blushed with pleasure. ''Tis nothing,' she insisted. 'What colour would you like, mistress?'

'What do you think, Gwyneth?' asked Marion le Fevre. 'This blue is so pretty, but there's green, or yellow . . . What would Eleanor like best, do you think?'

'Blue will match her eyes, mistress,' Gwyneth replied.

'So it will! Blue it shall be.'

While Mistress Flax took out her rod to measure the linen, Gwyneth looked around for Hereward. She didn't see him, but she caught sight of Bedwyn the stonemason coming away from Rhys Freeman's shop. He towered above the rest of the villagers, who cleared a way for him like reeds parting beneath a scythe.

Quickly excusing herself to Marion, Gwyneth hurried towards the silent man and met him at the edge of the market stalls. Bedwyn's shoulders were hunched as if he could feel the unfriendly glances like blows, his eyes on the ground and his face hidden by his tangle of dark hair.

'Master Bedwyn, how is your hand?'

The huge man looked up with a start. Then his eyes brightened and he smiled. He held up his injured hand, and Gwyneth saw that it was neatly bandaged.

'Brother Padraig dressed it for you?' The man nodded. 'Does it hurt much?' A shake of the head. 'I'm sure it will soon be better,' smiled Gwyneth.

Bedwyn gave her the strange courtly bow that she had seen before. Gwyneth felt as if she should curtsy in return, but before she could move she felt someone grab her arm, and turned to see Margery Carver.

'Gwyneth Mason! Whatever do you think you're doing?' The carpenter's wife's voice was high-pitched with annoyance. 'It's not safe talking to him.'

Bedwyn's smile vanished. Head bowed, he turned away and strode down the street.

'Goodbye, Bedwyn!' Gwyneth called after him. 'I'm glad your hand is better.'

The stonemason didn't respond. As he drew level with the linen weaver's stall, Gwyneth noticed Marion le Fevre put one hand to her head and reach out to support herself. Was she ill? Gwyneth wondered anxiously.

She wanted to hurry across to her, but Margery Carver was still hanging on to her arm. 'What would your mother think if I told her what you're doing?' she demanded, giving her an angry little shake.

'Mother teaches us to be polite.' Gwyneth felt her temper start to rise. 'There's nothing to be afraid of. Bedwyn is a kind man.'

'And what would you know about it, young mistress? You've only to look at the size of him to know there's something less than holy about him. Nobody knows who he is or where he comes from.' Mistress Carver crossed herself vigorously. 'God grant we're not all murdered in our beds!'

'Nay, mistress.' A measured, deep voice broke into the conversation as Tom Smith, the local blacksmith, turned away from Mistress Carver's stall with a wooden bowl in one hand. 'We have heard nothing villainous of Bedwyn.'

'No good, either,' Margery Carver snapped back at him. She flapped her hands at Gwyneth. 'Be off home with you, or I will tell your mother!'

Keeping her lips pressed tightly together,

Gwyneth turned away. As she went, she caught a wink from Tom Smith, which helped her feel a little better, but there were reproving looks from other villagers as she made her way back to Mistress Flax's stall.

The weaver was folding up the piece of blue linen. She shook her head at Gwyneth and clicked her tongue, but said nothing. Marion le Fevre was nowhere in sight.

'Where's Mistress le Fevre?' Gwyneth asked.

Before Mistress Flax could reply the stall swayed, and Gwyneth realized that Marion le Fevre was half concealed among the lengths of fabric, clinging to one of the wooden supports with the other hand still pressed to her head.

'Mistress le Fevre, what's the matter?' she cried.

'My head—oh, child, my head hurts terribly! Here.' The embroideress fumbled at her girdle and drew out her purse. 'Pay Mistress Flax for me, please. I must go back to the Crown immediately.'

Gwyneth took the purse and counted out some coins into Mistress Flax's hand. Taking the linen in exchange, she saw that Hereward had reappeared with a laden basket. 'Have you finished?' she asked, laying the fabric neatly on top of the other purchases. 'Mistress le Fevre is ill. We must take her home right away.'

Marion leant heavily on Gwyneth as they led her away. She stumbled several times as if she could hardly see where she was going, and she kept uttering little gasps of pain.

'We're here now,' Gwyneth said comfortingly as they turned underneath the arch into the inn yard. 'Soon you can rest.'

Before they reached the door of the inn, Idony Mason came hurrying out. 'Mistress le Fevre, what is it?'

The embroideress looked ready to faint, and it was Gwyneth who explained, 'She said her head hurts. It came on all of a sudden.'

Idony's eyes widened with concern. Taking Gwyneth's place at the embroideress's side, she said, 'Come with me, mistress. I'll turn down your bed so you can lie down, and send for some hot bricks. And I'll brew you a posset to help you sleep. You'll soon be right as rain.'

'So kind . . .' Marion le Fevre murmured as Idony led her away.

'I wonder what the matter is?' Gwyneth said, watching them go. 'If mother's posset doesn't work, we'll have to send for Brother Padraig.'

'I expect she—' Hereward began.

The sound of running footsteps interrupted him. Spinning round, Gwyneth saw their friends Ivo and Amabel Thorson, the sheriff's children, dashing through the archway. Their usually mischievous faces were filled with fear and anxiety.

'What is it?' Gwyneth exclaimed.

'Father sent us,' Amabel gasped. 'They've searched the abbey, and no one can find her anywhere!'

'Who?' Hereward asked in confusion.

'It's Eleanor FitzStephen,' Ivo replied. 'She's disappeared!'

Chapter Four

'What? Eleanor missing?' Gwyneth couldn't believe it. 'But we only saw her yesterday!'

'Well, she is,' said Ivo. He was red-faced and panting, and had to pause before he went on. 'Lord Ralph just came to tell father, and he sent us to tell the rest of the village.'

'What happened?' Hereward demanded.

'No one knows,' Amabel replied. 'Lord Ralph said that her nursemaid put Eleanor to bed last night, but when she went to wake her this morning she was gone. She was nowhere in Lord Ralph's lodgings, so they searched the whole of the abbey grounds. She isn't there.'

'She'll turn up.' Hereward was trying to sound confident, though Gwyneth could see that he was anxious. 'She'll be in someone's house, stuffing sweetmeats, or . . . well, somewhere. I'll tell father,' he called over his shoulder, leaving his basket on the ground and running back across the inn yard.

'If you find Eleanor, take her back to the abbey, and let father know,' Amabel said. Without giving Gwyneth a chance to ask anything else, she and Ivo dashed out through the archway.

Gwyneth heaved up the basket and went into the inn. Her mother and father were talking anxiously by the door to the taproom.

'That poor child!' said Idony. 'If she's lost she'll be so frightened.'

'I'm sure she's not here,' Geoffrey Mason said, 'but I'll search the place to be sure. Gwyneth, you and Hereward had better go and help look in the village. Wat and Hankin—' he named the inn's two servants— 'can go as well. Any news?' he asked as Hereward appeared, panting.

'I checked the stables, father. She's not there. Perhaps she came to visit Mistress le Fevre?'

'I don't think she would do that,' Gwyneth said. 'She was shy of Marion, remember?'

'Mistress le Fevre is lying down with the shutters closed,' said Idony. 'And I've a posset to brew for her. I'll check her room when I take it up. Best not tell her yet, though—the news will only upset her.'

She disappeared into the kitchen and Gwyneth heard pots rattling. Geoffrey went back into the taproom, calling loudly for Wat and Hankin.

'Come on,' said Hereward. 'Let's go and look. Where do you think Eleanor might have gone?'

Gwyneth shook her head helplessly. 'Surely nowhere, without someone seeing her?' The little girl was a favourite in the village and she would have been welcome in anyone's house, but she was never allowed to run around without her nursemaid. None of the villagers was likely to let her stay without sending a message to her father at the abbey.

'Her father took her to Tom Smith's forge last week to watch his horse being shod,' Hereward said. 'She liked that. We could start there, anyway.'

Gwyneth knew that if Eleanor had turned up at the forge Mari Smith would have taken her home right away, but she had no better idea. She and Hereward went out into the street again. A hubbub of anxious chatter from the market-place told Gwyneth that the twins had spread the message there, so she and Hereward turned in the other direction, past Finn Thorson's house. The sheriff was standing just outside his door, talking to Brother Barnabas, the abbey steward. As Gwyneth and Hereward went past, Godfrey de Massard came riding up on his magnificent black stallion. He drew rein beside Master Thorson and bent down to speak to him. For once his chilly grey eyes looked concerned.

'I'll ride out on the road to Wells and search there,' he said. 'Most likely Eleanor is still in the village, but who knows where the child might have strayed?'

'True, Father Godfrey,' Brother Barnabas replied. 'You have our thanks.'

Godfrey de Massard raised a hand in farewell and spurred his horse into a brisk trot. Gwyneth watched him heading up the street as she and Hereward followed more slowly.

'I wouldn't have expected Father Godfrey to help,' she said, and added reluctantly, 'Maybe he's not so bad after all.'

Hereward grunted and said nothing. The abbey bell began to ring for terce as Father Godfrey disappeared. Brother Barnabas hastily said goodbye to Finn Thorson and crossed the street towards the abbey gate.

'Mid-morning already,' Gwyneth murmured. 'Eleanor has been missing for hours.'

As they rounded the street corner, and the forge came into sight, Gwyneth saw that the news had got there first. Tom and his brother

Hywel were carefully lifting logs off the wood-pile.

Hywel straightened up and called a greeting to them, his blue eyes round with worry. 'We thought the little maid might have crawled in here,' he explained.

'But she hasn't, praise God,' his brother added, tossing another log out of the way. He gave the scattered wood a look of disgust. 'Better get this lot stacked up again.'

Just then, Tom's wife Mari poked her head out of an upstairs window and called down, 'She's not here, Tom.'

There was no point in staying longer. Gwyneth and Hereward went on, past the back gate of the abbey and along the abbey wall as far as the crossroads beside Chalcwelle, and then along Tor Lane to return to the centre of the village from the other direction.

People were searching everywhere. Gwyneth and Hereward heard Eleanor's name being called over and over again, but never a reply. They did the best they could, searching under bushes and down alleyways between houses, but every thicket and every cranny in the walls was empty.

At last they came to the corner opposite Rhys

Freeman's shop. Ivo and Amabel were coming out of his front door, closely followed by the shopkeeper himself. 'You've no call to come poking through my private things,' he was saying crossly. 'I told you the young maid's not here.'

'We were just making sure,' Ivo replied.

Gwyneth's heart suddenly began to beat faster. Rhys Freeman was the most unfriendly man in the village; she wouldn't have put it past him to keep Eleanor shut up somewhere. What was more, his cellar had hidden dark secrets once— the fake relics which Rhys Freeman made and sold, and the bones of King Arthur which he had stolen from the abbey.

'Maybe we'd better check your cellar,' Ivo added, as if he could read Gwyneth's thoughts.

'Young limb of Satan,' Rhys Freeman grumbled, but he detached a key from his belt and opened the door in the side wall of his shop which led into his cellar. 'Might as well build a thoroughfare to London through the place and have done with it,' he muttered.

Gwyneth and Hereward crowded round to look as Ivo plunged down the steps shouting, 'Eleanor! Eleanor!'

He reappeared a moment later, brushing dust and cobwebs off the front of his tunic. 'Nothing but spiders,' he reported, with a disgusted look on his face. 'Master Freeman, don't you ever take a broom down there?'

'I'll take a broom to you if you don't be off,' Rhys Freeman threatened, locking the door again. 'I haven't seen Eleanor and I don't know where she's gone.'

Gwyneth and Hereward turned for home with the twins. There was a cold, hard feeling in the pit of Gwyneth's stomach. As time went by and Eleanor still wasn't found, it became more and more likely that she was really lost, or lying hurt somewhere.

Outside the abbey gateway, Lord Ralph FitzStephen was talking to a group of men with poles in their hands. His face looked haggard with worry, but he addressed the men vigorously, pointing to each road that led out of the village. The men saluted him and hurried off, some down the road that led to the Tor, others towards the bridge over the river.

'It's almost mid-day,' said Hereward, glancing at the sun. 'We should fetch the food for the stonemasons and take it to the abbey.'

'But we have to look for Eleanor,' Gwyneth objected.

'Tasks don't do themselves,' said Hereward, practical as ever. 'And lots of people are searching.'

Amabel said, 'We'll go home too, and see if there's any news. If there is, we'll come and tell you.'

The friends parted outside the door of the Crown. Idony Mason had the basket of food and skin of ale ready outside the kitchen. 'Tell Lord Ralph there's no news yet,' she said. 'But we'll keep looking.'

The bell for the service of sext began to ring as Gwyneth hauled her basket under the abbey gateway, followed by Hereward with the ale. The first person she saw was their friend Brother Timothy on his way to the chapel, and she set down the basket so that she could hurry forward and meet him. 'Brother Timothy, is there any more news?'

The young monk looked down at her, his bony features solemn. 'News of Eleanor? No, nothing yet. We will pray for her, Gwyneth.'

He had to go, answering the summons of the bell, leaving Gwyneth to stare after him with a feeling close to despair.

Hereward jerked his head in the direction of the half-built church. 'Everything's quiet there. Maybe the workmen are searching as well.'

Gwyneth realized that he was right. She could not hear the familiar sound of chisels clinking on stone, as if they had slipped back to the time before the discovery of Arthur's bones, when work had stopped because there was no money to pay for building materials.

But as she passed through a half-finished doorway, she saw that the workmen were not out looking for Eleanor. Lord Ralph FitzStephen was standing with his back to her, the stone-masons clustered around him. Eleanor's nurse-maid Hilde was there, clutching the kitten and weeping into its fur.

'We must search the marshes and drag the river.' Lord Ralph's voice was tightly controlled. 'I have ordered all the villagers with boats to come to the landing stage. Will you join us and help?'

There was a murmur of agreement from the assembled men. Owen Mason said, 'We're with you, my lord. But there's no call to think of dragging the river yet. Eleanor will be found.'

'Oh, God help the child!' Hilde sobbed. 'There are evil men in the woods, or wild beasts and—'

'No need to speak of that,' Lord Ralph snapped. He swung round when he heard Gwyneth and Hereward approaching. Hope lit his face, which faded when he saw that Eleanor was not with them. 'Eat quickly, and meet me at the abbey gate,' he said to the stonemasons, brushing past Gwyneth with the nursemaid stumbling after him.

'The man suffers,' Owen Mason said sombrely, watching him go.

There was nothing Gwyneth could say. Quickly she began to distribute bread, cold beef, and cheese to the workmen, who ate where they stood, while Hereward poured ale into horn beakers.

'She'd surely not go as far as the marshes.' Matt Green spoke round a mouthful of cheese. 'Eleanor was a good little maid. She'd not wander away on her own.'

His words struck a chill through Gwyneth. Master Green was right; Eleanor might be mischievous, but she would never deliberately worry the people who loved her. She had been missing since the early morning, or even the night before. That must mean that she was lying hurt somewhere—Gwyneth did not want to believe that she might be dead—or that someone had taken her away.

She was looking round for Hereward, when she saw that Bedwyn was approaching her. Bowing, he held out a chunk of amber hanging from a leather cord. The autumn sun caught it and woke a golden glow within its depths.

'That's beautiful!' Gwyneth exclaimed.

Bedwyn pointed to the bandage on his hand, then to the amber necklace, and offered it to her again.

'For me?' Gwyneth said. 'Oh, but, Bedwyn, I can't. I didn't do anything.'

The silent man smiled at her, his whole face lightening. For a moment Gwyneth saw behind the tangle of dark hair and the rough workman's clothing, and realized that once he must have been a very different kind of man. What had happened to him? she wondered. What had he suffered, that he could not speak and went around with that grim look that so many of the villagers found frightening?

Very gently, Bedwyn placed the leather cord round Gwyneth's neck, lifting her hair so that he could settle it in place. Then he bowed again, and for an instant she felt like a queen.

'Thank you, sir,' she said, curtsying.

Around them, the workmen were finishing their meal and beginning to make their way towards the abbey gates. Bedwyn went with them as Hereward came up to Gwyneth.

'Let's leave the basket and the skins here,' he said. 'Father won't mind waiting for them today. We can go and help search in the marshes.'

Agreeing, Gwyneth followed him to the abbey gateway, where the stonemasons were gathering around Ralph FitzStephen. Finn Thorson was there, and Godfrey de Massard had returned, still mounted on his black stallion. More of the villagers were waiting, too, including Ivo and Amabel, who for once had serious looks on their freckled faces.

When all the stonemasons had arrived, Finn Thorson raised his voice. 'Split into three groups. One to the boats by the landing stage, one to search the marshes between here and the Tor, and one to go upstream towards Wearyall Hill. Take poles to prod the pools and the bushes. If you find anything, come back here. Lord Ralph will stay to wait for news.'

'No,' Lord Ralph protested hoarsely. 'I'm going with the search party.'

'It's all right, I'll stay,' said Godfrey de Massard.

Lord Ralph flashed him a grateful look, though Gwyneth wondered uncharitably if the aristocratic priest had made the offer so that he didn't have to get his fine woollen habit covered in mud from the marshes.

'Right, then,' said Finn Thorson. 'Report to Father Godfrey if you see anything—Eleanor herself, of course, or her clothes, or—'

'She had her doll with her,' Lord Ralph put in. His voice shook. 'She never went anywhere without her doll.'

Master Thorson rested a hand on the man's shoulder. 'We'll find her,' he promised. Raising his voice, he went on, 'Go now, and don't give up until dark.'

'And may God go with you,' added Father Godfrey, raising his hand in a sign of blessing.

As the men began milling around in the abbey gateway, dividing themselves into the three groups Finn Thorson had asked for, Gwyneth was thrust close to Lord Ralph. Glancing at her, he began, 'Gwyneth, can you and Hereward—' then broke off, staring.

He reached out and touched the chunk of amber that hung round her neck on its cord.

'Where did you get this?' he asked in a whisper.

Before Gwyneth could reply, his fingers clenched tight around the stone. 'This is Eleanor's!' he went on, his voice rising to a shout. 'Where did you get it?'

Chapter Five

Lord Ralph was clutching the necklace cord so tightly that Gwyneth could hardly breathe. His face was white, his mouth set in a hard line and his dark eyes boring into hers.

'Where did you get it?' he repeated. He jerked the cord and it gave way with a snap, stinging Gwyneth's neck. 'Tell me, girl—don't stand there gaping!'

Gwyneth choked as she fought for breath. 'Bedwyn gave it to me,' she said when she could speak.

An angry muttering rose all around them and the huge workman was pushed to the front of the crowd.

Lord Ralph thrust out his hand with the chunk of amber. 'Where did you get this?'

Bedwyn shook his head, his eyes growing wide with alarm.

'Tell me the truth, man. Are you denying you gave it to Gwyneth here?'

Bedwyn shook his head again. Gwyneth dug her nails into her palms. Even though she knew Bedwyn was unable to speak, it looked as though he was deliberately refusing to answer Lord Ralph. Dreadful fears crowded into her mind; was it possible that Bedwyn knew where Eleanor was?

'Then tell me what you know of Eleanor!' Lord Ralph grabbed Bedwyn by the arms. The slender man was dwarfed by the mason, but he looked ready to attack him with his bare hands. 'What have you done with her?'

'Wait, wait.' Finn Thorson's calm voice interrupted as he pushed himself between Bedwyn and the furious Lord Ralph. 'My lord, he cannot speak. We must question him carefully. Bedwyn, did you give this necklace to Gwyneth?'

Bedwyn nodded and the crowd surged forward. 'Child stealer!' someone shouted.

Gwyneth wondered whether Bedwyn realized the danger he was in. She flashed a look at Hereward, who had wriggled to the front of the crowd, but her brother's gaze was fixed on the massive stonemason.

'Where did you get it?' Finn Thorson went on. 'No, that won't do . . . wait. Did you find it?' Another nod from Bedwyn. 'Where? In the abbey grounds?' Bedwyn shook his head. 'In the village?' He shook his head again.

'In the woods?' Finn Thorson tried again at the same time as Lord Ralph, unable to keep quiet any longer, burst out with, 'Have you seen Eleanor?'

Bedwyn nodded, and a roar of outrage rose up from the listening crowd.

'Where—where?' Lord Ralph asked.

Bedwyn's face took on a look of strain, as if he was desperately trying to speak, but no words would come.

'Hang him!' someone cried from the back of the crowd. 'He's done away with her, for sure!'

'No!' Gwyneth darted in front of the stone-mason as if she could protect him from the anger of the mob. 'He didn't say he'd seen Eleanor. He meant he found the necklace in the woods! Didn't you, Bedwyn?'

Bedwyn nodded furiously. But no one, except perhaps for Finn Thorson, was taking notice of him or listening to Gwyneth. More furious shouts rose from the crowd, as if they wanted to fall on

Bedwyn and execute him then and there. The stonemason was looking round at them, his expression darkening. His hand strayed to his belt—almost as if he expected to find a sword there, Gwyneth thought. Finding nothing, he let his hand fall back to his side, and stood in front of the sheriff with his head bowed.

'This won't do,' said Sheriff Thorson. 'Bedwyn, you're under arrest. The rest of you—' raising his voice—'get to your search. We still have to find Eleanor.'

Most of the crowd began to obey but a few of the villagers remained, headed by Dickon Carver, the village carpenter.

'We'll come with you, Master Thorson,' he said. 'Just to make sure you get him safely under lock and key. That's a dangerous man.'

'Very well,' Finn Thorson said, 'but if any of you lay a finger on him, I'll arrest you as well. We'll do this according to law.'

Master Carver spat. 'Law! We all *know* what he did. Why don't you string him up and have done with it?'

'Use your head, Dickon Carver,' Finn Thorson retorted. 'If he's guilty, he's the only man who knows what happened to Eleanor. And you want him dead before he can tell us? Your wits are addled!'

Master Carver stepped back with a sheepish look. 'Well, perhaps,' he admitted grudgingly. 'But we'll still come with you and make sure he's locked up. None of our wives and children are safe.'

'Please yourself,' said the sheriff. He put a hand on Bedwyn's shoulder and began to walk him down the street.

Gwyneth hurried to keep pace with Finn Thorson on his other side. 'Please, Master Thorson, don't take him,' she begged. 'I'm *sure* he didn't hurt Eleanor. He meant to say he found the necklace in the woods.'

'Perhaps he did, but none of us can be sure,' Finn Thorson replied, though he looked sympathetic. 'Would I be doing my job if I let him roam free round the village? Besides,' he added, 'it's for his own safety. What would the village men do to him, do you think, if they could get at him?'

Gwyneth had to admit that he was right. She turned back towards the abbey gate, where the last of the men were dividing themselves into groups. Standing a little further up the street, in the shadow cast by the abbey wall, she spotted a familiar brown-robed figure.

She stiffened. 'Ursus!'

The hermit had not seen her. He was staring after Finn Thorson and Bedwyn with a look of pure shock on his face. When Gwyneth called out to him again, he seemed to come to himself, turned away, and began walking rapidly towards the corner of the street.

'Ursus, wait!' She broke into a run, but the hermit rounded the street corner before she could catch him up, and when she reached it he was nowhere to be seen. She jumped as someone tapped her shoulder.

'What's the matter?' Hereward asked.

'I saw Ursus, but now he's gone.'

'Not again!' Hereward's face mirrored Gwyneth's own frustration. 'We still need to ask him about herbs for Edmund.'

'And I bet he would know all the best places to look for Eleanor,' Gwyneth said.

'He may be looking already,' Hereward suggested. 'If he's been in the village, he's bound to have heard. Do you want to go and join the search in the marshes?'

Gwyneth shook her head. After all the stress

and activity of the morning, she felt worn out. Besides, she was sure the searchers would not find anything. The answer to the mystery of where Eleanor had gone was locked in Bedwyn's head, and the stonemason was locked in a cell where no one could ask the right questions to solve it.

Gwyneth tapped on Marion le Fevre's door and balanced her tray in one hand so that she could lift the latch with the other. Idony had sent up some of the best white bread, with a little cold chicken and a cup of French wine to tempt the embroideress's appetite.

Marion le Fevre was lying on the bed, propped up by pillows, with her hair loose on her shoulders. Her face was pale and she looked weary, though she still gave Gwyneth her wonderful smile.

'Oh, thank you!' she exclaimed as Gwyneth settled the tray on her lap. 'How kind you are.'

'I'm glad to see you're feeling better,' said Gwyneth.

'A little.' Marion pressed her fingers to her forehead. 'My head still aches, and my throat is sore, but I think I could manage some of that delicious chicken.'

'Would you like me to send for Brother Padraig?' Gwyneth offered. 'I'm sure he would have a remedy for what ails you.'

'Brother Padraig? No, no,' Marion replied. 'This will pass.'

Gwyneth's aunt, Anne Mason, turned from the window where she was assembling a second embroidery frame next to the first one. 'Have they found that poor child yet?' she asked.

Gwyneth cast an uneasy glance at Marion, who said, 'Don't worry, child. I know about Eleanor. Who would have thought this would happen, when I bought that pretty linen for her gown?' She sighed.

'We haven't found her,' Gwyneth replied to her aunt. 'But everyone thinks Bedwyn took her away. Finn Thorson has arrested him.'

Marion le Fevre sat up, her lips parted as if to ask a question, but before she could speak Anne Mason interrupted.

'I knew it!' she exclaimed. She was a small, energetic woman with bright eyes like a bird's; they were flashing with anger now. 'I knew that man would have something to do with it!'

'But, aunt, you couldn't possibly know that!' Gwyneth protested.

'Oh, couldn't I?' Anne Mason had gone pink with indignation. 'I'll have you know, last night when your uncle Owen came home he told me Bedwyn had stayed on the site to finish off dressing a block of stone. Hardworking, he said!' She let out a scornful laugh. 'Hardworking? It was just an excuse to stay at the abbey and steal that poor child out of her bed.'

'It would seem so,' Marion commented gravely and sank back against her pillows. 'Though it grieves me to believe ill of anyone.'

'Well, someone took the child!' Anne pointed out. 'And now we know who, though I fear it's too late to save her.' She put down the piece of the frame she had been holding and went on, 'If you'll excuse me, mistress, I'll just slip round to Finn Thorson's and tell him what Owen told me. He ought to know.'

'Aunt Anne, that doesn't prove anything!' Gwyneth tried to protest again, but her aunt ignored her. She went out in a rustle of skirts, and the door closed behind her with a decided snap. 'Mistress le Fevre, I'm sure it wasn't Bedwyn,' Gwyneth said despairingly, turning back to the woman on the pillows.

'But who else?' Marion took a sip of wine, her

huge eyes gazing sorrowfully at Gwyneth over the rim of the cup. 'No one in the village would harm a hair of the poor child's head. And how much do we know about this stonemason?'

'Well, I don't believe it!' Gwyneth would never have imagined until now that she could feel angry with the beautiful embroideress. 'Bedwyn is a gentle man.'

Marion le Fevre fluttered one long-fingered hand towards her. 'Child, child, your faith does you credit. But I doubt that Bedwyn deserves it.'

Gwyneth tightened her lips, keeping back a furious retort. When she could trust her voice, she said, 'I know Bedwyn does not come often to the village, but Uncle Owen said there was nothing to fear from him. I cannot believe that he has hurt Eleanor until someone finds some real proof.'

She dropped a flustered curtsy to Marion before turning to leave, ignoring the embroideress as she called out, 'Gwyneth, my dear!'

Seething with silent anger, Gwyneth went downstairs. When she reached the kitchen door it opened and her mother looked out.

'There you are!' Idony exclaimed. 'Come and

wash your hands. There's a batch of bread ready for kneading.'

Gwyneth followed her mother into the kitchen. It was a relief to stand among the warm, homely smells of cooking, and even more to pummel the bread dough, imagining it was all the stupid people who were ready to believe the worst of Bedwyn when there was no real proof at all.

'We've got to do something,' she muttered to herself.

'What?' The voice was Hereward's.

Gwyneth glanced round to see him coming in from the yard with a basket of eggs. She motioned for him to join her, with one eye on their mother who was standing on the other side of the kitchen adding spices to a pot of frumenty that was simmering over the fire.

Hereward set the basket down. 'Are you still worrying about Bedwyn?'

'Someone has to,' Gwyneth replied. 'If we can't prove that he's innocent, then Finn Thorson will hang him.'

Hereward looked at her with a frown, and Gwyneth felt something cold clutch at her heart. She guessed what her brother was going to say an instant before he said it.

'But, Gwyneth, are we so sure that he *is* innocent?'

'Not you as well!' Gwyneth exclaimed in dismay.

'We don't know anything about Bedwyn,' Hereward pointed out. 'He never worked on the abbey site until the other day. Perhaps he is the kind of man who would hurt a little girl.'

'No he's not, I'm sure he's not.' To her horror, Gwyneth heard her voice begin to shake. Struggling to control herself, she went on, 'It's wrong to hang him without any real proof.'

'He had Eleanor's necklace,' Hereward reminded her.

'He said he found it. He could be telling the truth. Hereward, we have to do something.' Determination welled up inside Gwyneth and she squeezed the bread dough until it popped out between her fingers in little worms. 'We found out what happened to King Arthur's bones, and the cross. We can find out about this as well.'

To her annoyance Hereward looked doubtful. 'And what if we find proof that Bedwyn did take Eleanor away?'

'Very well. I'd believe it if we found proof— but we won't find it, because he *didn't*!' Gwyneth raised her voice and then lowered it again as her mother glanced round from stirring the pot. 'Hereward, can't you see that this is wrong? Don't you want to help him?'

'Not if he's a murderer.' Hereward was looking just as determined. 'The first thing we have to do is find Eleanor.'

'The whole village is looking for Eleanor!' Gwyneth said. 'But no one is trying to find out what really happened. No one cares, not even you. And if you won't help, I'll do it myself!'

Giving the bread a last vicious thump, she whirled round and ran out of the kitchen.

Chapter Six

Gwyneth paused under the archway that led into the street, wiping traces of bread dough from her hands onto her apron. Looking up, she saw a small knot of villagers clustered around the door of Finn Thorson's house. Somebody yelled, 'Bring him out! Hang him!' and someone else threw a stone that banged on the door and rebounded.

Gwyneth noticed a couple of strangers—pilgrims by the look of their hats and staffs—skirting the crowd with uneasy looks.

Yet more trouble! she thought with a sigh. It was the last thing the village needed now that the pilgrims were beginning to return. No one would want to stay in Glastonbury with all this going on.

Suddenly the door to the sheriff's house opened and Finn Thorson came out. 'Stop this! Go back to your homes.'

Dickon Carver stepped out of the crowd and faced the sheriff. 'We'll go home when that murderer is punished.'

'Then you'll have a long wait,' the sheriff replied calmly. 'There'll be no punishment until Bedwyn has had a fair trial.'

A chorus of protest broke out. Rhys Freeman made his voice heard above the rest. 'And what's all this doing to our trade? Have you thought of that, Master Thorson? Who'll come here if they think a murderer is walking around loose?'

'If what you say about the stonemason is true, then he isn't loose,' Finn Thorson pointed out. 'He's locked up in my cellar and there he'll stay until his trial.'

'And how long will that be?' asked Matt Green the stonemason.

Finn Thorson shook his head. 'I can't tell you, Master Green. The most important thing is to find Eleanor.' His eyes darkened. 'You men would all be better employed searching for her, rather than standing out here in the street.'

'That brute hasn't left her alive,' Dickon Carver insisted. 'And Lord Ralph is the king's steward. What will King Richard think of Glastonbury when he comes home?'

A hush fell on the crowd, and Finn Thorson took advantage of it to repeat his order that the men should go home. Gradually they began to move away, muttering. Gwyneth hovered, wondering whether to ask the sheriff if she might talk to Bedwyn. A moment's thought convinced her that he would never allow it.

What can I do? she asked herself. She refused to go back into the Crown and face Hereward. Then she realized that there was one person above all others who might be able to help her. Resolutely, she turned her back on the sheriff's house and began to hurry down the street towards the Tor.

Gwyneth lifted her skirts and hopped from one tussock of grass to the next as she tried to make her way dry-shod through the marshes. The sun was going down; if she did not find Ursus soon it would be dark, and she would have to admit defeat and go home.

'Ursus, *please* be here this time,' she whispered.

She rounded a bramble thicket and came out onto the river bank, not far from the place where Rhys Freeman set his eel traps. Ursus was seated underneath a tree a little way upstream, watching a heron stalk through the shallows. Suddenly, the bird stabbed down into the water and came up with a silver fish gleaming in its beak.

The hermit turned to Gwyneth and held out a hand, smiling.

She ran towards him, forgetting to pick her way carefully over the boggy ground in her gladness at seeing him. 'Ursus!' she exclaimed. 'Oh, Ursus, I've wanted to talk to you so much.'

Ursus raised his brows enquiringly; unlike Bedwyn, he could speak, but he hoarded words as if they were made of gold.

'You were there in the village when they arrested Bedwyn the stonemason,' Gwyneth said, squatting down on the bank beside the hermit and speaking in a rush. 'They say he killed Lord Ralph's little daughter Eleanor, but I don't think he did. I'm afraid they'll hang him.'

Meeting Ursus's eyes, she saw that they were kind and full of wisdom. When he still said nothing, she went on to explain how Eleanor had been found missing from her bed, how Bedwyn had stayed late in the abbey grounds to finish his work, and how he had given her Eleanor's necklace.

'But I still can't believe it,' she finished. 'I think Bedwyn's a good man.'

'You see clearly,' Ursus said.

'But no one listens to me—not even Hereward!'

'They listened to you once,' the hermit pointed out, 'when you brought the buried cross back to the abbey.'

'But then we had the cross to show them,' said Gwyneth. 'And it was you who helped us to find it. You don't know where I could find proof that Bedwyn is innocent?' she added hopefully.

To her disappointment, Ursus shook his head. 'Alas, no. But if you truly believe it in your heart, you must go on searching.'

Gwyneth found herself encouraged by his understanding and the certainty in his voice. She got to her feet and curtsied. 'Thank you, sir. I will do so.'

'And is that all you wish to ask me?'

Gwyneth suddenly remembered the first reason why she and Hereward had come searching for the hermit; her anxiety for Eleanor and Bedwyn had almost driven it from her mind.

'No—there's Edmund Hardwycke as well. He's a child, sir, and he suffers terribly from the falling sickness. Do you know of any herbs that will help him? Brother Padraig couldn't do anything, and his father is afraid he'll die soon.'

Her voice faltered as she remembered her farewell to Edmund, and how bravely he accepted his illness even though he knew how short his life might be.

Ursus's face grew shadowed, and for an instant Gwyneth's heart thumped hard as she waited for him to say that nothing could help Edmund. Then he nodded. 'There are herbs that might help, though they are rare and hard to find. I will search for them on the slopes of the Tor. Come here tomorrow at this hour, and if God has guided me I will give them to you.'

'Thank you, sir!' Rather guiltily Gwyneth remembered Marion le Fevre, and how she had stormed out of her room when the embroideress refused to believe that Bedwyn might be innocent. 'Do you know of herbs for a headache and sore throat? One of our guests at the Crown is ill and has taken to her bed.'

'Certainly. I will search for herbs for her, too.'

Gwyneth thanked him again and turned to go. Ursus stretched out a hand to delay her. 'Do you remember what I told you when you were searching for the cross?' His eyes were very serious. 'Everything has its proper time to be found. If proof of Bedwyn's innocence exists, I believe that you will find it.'

Chapter Seven

'What's the matter with Gwyneth?' asked Idony Mason, turning away from stirring the pot of frumenty. 'Have you two had a quarrel?'

Hereward shifted his feet uncomfortably. He hadn't meant to quarrel with his sister, but she had flared up when he suggested that Bedwyn might be guilty. Once she got an idea into her head, it was hard to make her see reason.

'She's upset about Eleanor,' he explained. 'And Bedwyn.'

'So are we all.' Idony inspected the bread dough Gwyneth had been kneading, returned it to its earthenware bowl and spread a linen cloth over it. 'You'd better go and find her, Hereward. We can't have her dashing about the village in a state.'

Hereward scuffed his feet on an uneven flagstone. He didn't like to admit that he was partly responsible for Gwyneth running off, but he was glad to have a chance to look for her and make amends for their quarrel. He was as eager as his sister was to find out what they could about Eleanor's disappearance. He wasn't as sure as she was of Bedwyn's innocence, but he cared equally that the stonemason shouldn't hang for no reason. Maybe by now Gwyneth would have cooled down and they could make some plans.

There was no sign of his sister in the street outside. She would have gone to the abbey, Hereward guessed, or to the Tor in search of Ursus, so he set off in that direction. He ran through the gateway and took a quick look around the abbey precinct, but Gwyneth wasn't there either. A few of the stonemasons were back at work on the new church, but he guessed that most of them were still out looking for Eleanor.

As he was going out into the street again, a man stepped out from the shadow of the gateway. 'Good morrow, young master,' he said. 'Will you do an errand for me?'

He was a stranger, of medium height with neat grey hair and beard, wearing a brown tunic under a black cloak.

'If I can, sir,' Hereward replied. 'What is your errand?'

The man held out a sheet of parchment, folded and sealed. 'Take this letter and give it to Lord Ralph FitzStephen.'

'Yes, sir.' Hereward was anxious to get on with looking for Gwyneth, but at least the letter would give him the chance of seeing Lord Ralph and perhaps finding out more about Eleanor and Bedwyn.

He took the letter and the man walked off briskly down the street. The bell for nones began to ring and Hereward passed several monks making their way to the chapel as he headed for the guest lodgings where Lord Ralph was staying.

In the steward's rooms a bright fire had driven off the chill of the day. Lord Ralph was seated beside it with a cup of wine in his hand. Hereward thought he looked exhausted, and ten years older than he had done the day before. The seat on the other side of the fire was occupied by Godfrey de Massard.

Lord Ralph glanced up as Hereward came in. 'Oh, it's you, Hereward. What do you want?'

'I've brought you a letter, my lord.'

'Something to do with the building work, no doubt,' Lord Ralph said to Father Godfrey, and added, 'Wait for a moment, Hereward. I may need to send a reply.'

He got up and moved closer to the earthenware lamp, breaking the seal and spreading out the parchment so he could read it. Hereward saw his eyes widen and his face grow even whiter than before. He drew in a single rough breath and swayed, so that Father Godfrey sprang to his feet. Hereward stepped forward to grasp Lord Ralph's arm and steady him. Father Godfrey supported him on his other side, and together they eased the steward back into his chair.

'My lord, what is it?' asked the cleric, the firelight casting shadows across his face.

'Here, read it.' Lord Ralph flapped the letter at him, and when the priest took it he seized his wine cup from the table and swallowed the contents in one gulp.

'"To Lord Ralph FitzStephen",' Father Godfrey read aloud. '"Your daughter Eleanor is alive and well."' He stopped when he read the last words and stared at Lord Ralph, then went on hastily. '"She will be returned to you if you fill the abbey fish tank with gold and leave it in the woods near the road to Wells, in the clearing by the old stone cross. Be there at dusk three days from now, and say nothing to a soul if you wish to see your daughter alive again."'

Hereward felt an enormous bubble of joy swell inside him. Eleanor was alive! Eager to hear more, he retreated a pace towards the fire, hoping the two men would forget he was there.

Father Godfrey was smiling and there was warmth in his eyes, a look Hereward had never seen there before. 'My lord, this is wonderful news!' he said. 'Is three days enough to gather the gold?'

'Yes . . . yes.' Lord Ralph still looked stunned, but Hereward could see that his exhaustion was dissolving and his eyes were growing bright again. 'I must write straightway to my estates, and they will send it at once. And we can let the villagers know they can call off the search.'

'No, my lord.' Godfrey de Massard's smile vanished and he spoke sharply. 'See what it says in the letter. "Say nothing to a soul."'

Lord Ralph frowned. 'But the whole village is in fear for Eleanor. Must I keep from them the news that she is alive?'

'Yes, for Eleanor's sake. Think of her danger if you disobey the orders in the letter.'

Lord Ralph let out a sigh. 'You're right, of course, Father. We must do whatever is necessary to make sure she comes home safely.'

The priest rested a hand on his shoulder, but when he looked up at Hereward his grey eyes were cold. 'If word of this gets out, boy, you will answer to me.'

'Yes, sir,' Hereward replied at once. Brightening, he added, 'It won't be long before the ransom is paid. And then Bedwyn can go free.'

Both men turned to look at him, and Hereward realized too late that he should not have spoken so boldly.

'Not so fast, boy,' Father Godfrey warned. 'We still do not know what part the stonemason has played in this.'

'But Bedwyn is locked up in Master Thorson's cellar,' Hereward protested. 'It was someone quite different who gave me the letter, someone I've never seen before. Bedwyn must be innocent!'

Lord Ralph shook his head, and Father Godfrey frowned as if he was trying to explain something to a stupid novice. 'It proves no such thing, boy. All we can be sure of is that Bedwyn did not act alone. We have heard that he stayed late in the abbey grounds last night, and we know that he had Eleanor's necklace. He might not be a murderer, but he still has charges to answer.'

'But that's ridiculous!' Father Godfrey's brows arched, and Hereward felt hot with embarrassment. 'I'm sorry, sir. But if Bedwyn had taken Eleanor, he would never have given the necklace to my sister.'

'Who knows what he would have done?' said Lord Ralph. 'It's too early yet to talk of freeing him.'

'The man who gave you the letter,' Father Godfrey went on. 'What was he like?'

'Just an ordinary man, my lord,' Hereward replied. 'Middle sized, grey haired. He might have been a soldier,' he added, remembering the man's upright bearing.

'I'd wager he was,' said the priest, 'and I could make a good guess whose. My lord, this might be a plot of Henry of Truro.'

Lord Ralph looked startled, then nodded. 'You could be right. If he is planning rebellion, he will need gold.'

Hereward felt a spark of excitement. News had come to Glastonbury before of Henry of Truro, the cousin of King Richard. He had already been caught trying to kill the king and seize the crown for himself. Richard had pardoned him and sent him into exile in Wales, but now that Richard was far from England on his Crusade, Henry was plotting again. Rhys Freeman's fake relics had been used to raise money for the traitor; now that he had lost this source of funds, Henry must be looking for another.

'The plan is clear,' said Godfrey de Massard. 'Henry would recruit a man working at the abbey so that he could steal Eleanor away. Bedwyn is ideal—big and strong, and he cannot speak to reveal what he knows. And now that she is in his hands, Henry has sent this letter demanding gold.'

'And he shall have it,' said Lord Ralph. 'What else can I do, with Eleanor in danger?' His voice took on a raw edge as he added, 'Please God they do not harm her.'

'They will not,' Father Godfrey said soothingly. 'If Henry wants to make himself king, the last thing he needs is the reputation of slaughtering children. You will soon have Eleanor safely home again.'

'Yes, I will write at once. My man shall ride through the night.' Lord Ralph sprang to his feet and strode across the room to a table spread with writing materials. Passing Hereward, he clapped him on the shoulder. 'Thank you, boy. You have brought me rare news. Here.' He fumbled in the purse at his belt and pressed a silver penny into Hereward's hand. 'You may go now.'

'Thank you, my lord.'

Hereward desperately wanted to make them see how absurd it was that Bedwyn should be plotting with Henry of Truro, but Lord Ralph was already searching for a clean sheet of parchment, and Godfrey de Massard's face wore an unfriendly expression. 'Go,' he said, giving Hereward a stare from flinty grey eyes. 'And remember to say nothing.'

Daunted by the cleric's hard stare, Hereward bowed and left. As he closed the door behind him, he saw Father Godfrey go to Lord Ralph's side and look over his shoulder at what he was writing. Hereward drew the door shut, all but a tiny crack, and pressed himself against the wall to listen.

For a few moments there was nothing but the scratching of Lord Ralph's quill. Then Eleanor's father said, 'Enough gold to fill the abbey fish tank? I trust my steward has sufficient funds in ready money.' He sighed. 'I am not a wealthy man. When the ransom is paid, I will have barely enough to live on. I shall have to sell my dear wife's jewels if Eleanor is to have a dowry.' The pen scratched again. 'But it must be done. The fish tank must be filled.'

'The notion of the fish tank puzzles me, my lord,' said Father Godfrey. 'Why should they ask for that? Is it not made of stone, fixed in the kitchen, like the one we have at Wells?'

'No, it's a metal cauldron.' Lord Ralph spoke dismissively. 'A huge thing, but I can have it moved. More important is to get the gold.'

Silence again, except for the scratching of the pen. Suddenly Hereward heard Father Godfrey click his tongue. 'There's a vile draught. That careless boy has left the door open.'

With a stab of alarm, Hereward heard footsteps approach the door. He darted away to take refuge round the nearest corner of the passage. He heard the door bang shut and started to breathe more easily.

As he left the guest lodgings and hurried towards the abbey gate, he wanted to run and jump to let loose his excitement. Eleanor was alive and Bedwyn must be innocent, in spite of what Father Godfrey believed. Somehow there must be a way of proving it, or Bedwyn would hang as a traitor, if not a murderer.

Chapter Eight

Night was falling as Gwyneth returned to the Crown, and lamplight poured into the yard from the taproom window. The inn looked busy enough, though she could not hear the usual sound of cheerful talk and laughter from inside. Then Hereward appeared at the window and drew the shutters closed, leaving Gwyneth in darkness. She shivered in the frosty air and hurried across the cobbles to the door.

No one was in the kitchen; Gwyneth glanced into the taproom to see the benches half-filled with strangers wearing cloaks and cockleshell-shaped pilgrim badges among the villagers. All the familiar faces looked tired and discouraged, while the pilgrims seemed discomfited by the lack of cheer.

'We'll leave tomorrow,' Gwyneth heard one of them say to his wife. 'This is no place for Godfearing people.'

'Aye,' his wife replied. 'One of our children could be next.'

Gwyneth stopped wondering whether Eleanor might have been found while she was away; clearly the day's search had ended fruitlessly.

Her father was coming up from the cellar, helping Hankin to hoist a fresh barrel of ale up the steps. Idony Mason was serving out her frumenty, nodding and smiling as the guests dug into the fruity porridge. Hereward was distributing mugs of ale among the tables, but as soon as he saw Gwyneth he set down his tray and came across to grasp her arm and draw her into the empty kitchen.

'I looked for you, but I couldn't find you,' he began.

'I went to the Tor and spoke to Ursus,' Gwyneth explained, not sure yet if she and her brother were friends again. 'He said that I should go on searching for proof that Bedwyn is innocent. And he promised me some herbs for Edmund. I have to go back tomorrow to collect them.'

'That's good,' said Hereward. There was something about him that Gwyneth couldn't explain, a look of excitement gleaming in his eyes.

'Gwyneth, I'm sorry I didn't believe you earlier, when you said Bedwyn didn't hurt Eleanor. I don't think he did, now, and I want to help.'

Gwyneth knew how hard it was for anything to change Hereward's mind once he had made it up. 'What happened?' she asked.

Hereward opened his mouth to reply but then shook his head. 'I'm not supposed to tell anyone,' he said.

Irritated beyond measure, Gwyneth grabbed his shoulder and gave him a shake. 'I'm not "anyone". What happened?'

'All right. But you mustn't tell anyone else.' Hereward lowered his voice and moved away from the taproom door, motioning to Gwyneth to follow him. 'Eleanor is alive,' he announced in a low voice.

'What!' Gwyneth's voice squeaked in her amazement, and Hereward cast a glance towards the taproom door. 'How do you know? Why are you keeping it a secret?'

Hereward hastily explained to her about the letter he had taken to Lord Ralph FitzStephen, and the instructions it gave for Eleanor's ransom.

'Father Godfrey told me to keep silent, as the letter asked. Eleanor will be in danger if word gets out.'

'I won't say anything.' Gwyneth felt weak with relief at the thought that Eleanor would soon be returned to her father. 'It's hard for everyone to have to go on worrying and searching, but it won't be for long. It's far more important to get Eleanor home safely from whoever has stolen her.'

'But what can we do about Bedwyn?' Hereward asked. 'Father Godfrey is certain that he's one of Henry of Truro's men, but I can't believe it.'

'Of course he's not!' Gwyneth said scornfully. 'If he had stolen Eleanor away, he would have taken her to Henry and never come back to the abbey at all.'

'It's not even certain that this has anything to do with Henry of Truro,' Hereward reminded her. 'Father Godfrey thinks so, but then he thinks Henry is at the bottom of everything that goes wrong.' He grinned suddenly. 'If his horse went lame, he'd believe Henry of Truro did it!'

Gwyneth grinned back. It felt good to be on the same side as Hereward again.

'At least we don't have to worry about finding

Eleanor any more,' her brother went on thoughtfully. 'And once she comes home, she'll be able to tell everyone that it wasn't Bedwyn who took her.'

'That's if Eleanor knows who took her,' Gwyneth pointed out. A picture flew into her mind of a cloak being bundled over the little girl's head to muffle her cries as she was carried off.

Hereward nodded. 'You're right. And Finn Thorson doesn't know about the ransom letter. He might hang Bedwyn before Eleanor is released. Besides, Lord Ralph will have to give all the gold he has to get Eleanor back. If we could find out first—'

He stopped as their mother hurried in from the taproom with the empty pot.

'What are you two doing in here?' she asked sounding flustered. 'Hereward, your father wants you. Gwyneth, take that basket of bread and see everyone is served.'

Gwyneth glanced at Hereward. He was right; they couldn't just sit back and hope that everything would sort itself out. Bedwyn still needed their help, and tomorrow they would have to find a way to discover the truth.

★　★　★

Gwyneth felt nervous as she tapped at Marion le Fevre's door with her breakfast tray the next morning. She hadn't forgotten how she had stormed out of the room the day before. What if Mistress le Fevre wasn't yet ready to forgive her for her rudeness?

But when she heard Marion's voice and opened the door, there was a welcoming smile on the embroideress's face. Though she still looked pale, she was fully dressed, and sitting in a chair near the window.

'Put the tray down there, my dear,' she directed, gesturing towards the table. 'And then come here. I have something for you.' She held out a girdle made of plaited green silk and embroidered with gold thread.

'Oh, mistress!' Gwyneth gasped. 'That's too fine for me. And after I was so rude to you yesterday! I'm truly sorry.'

Marion le Fevre smiled. 'It's all forgotten, my dear. As for the girdle, 'tis no more than a trifle. Take it, I pray you.'

Gwyneth reached out and took the gift. The silk felt soft as lambswool in her fingers. 'It's beautiful! Thank you.'

'And now I shall have my breakfast and set to

work again,' Mistress le Fevre declared.

'Are you better today, mistress?'

Marion smiled bravely. 'Almost, my dear. Well enough to work at least, though not to go out, I fear. Your aunt will come later to help me.'

She rose to go to the table, and her eyes fell on the blue linen she had bought for Eleanor. She sighed and let her fingers trail over the surface of the fabric. 'Who knows if I will ever stitch the gown for her?' she murmured.

A wave of guilt swept over Gwyneth, and she wished she could tell Marion that Eleanor was safe and soon to be ransomed by her father. Fleeing from temptation to tell what she knew, she dropped a quick curtsy and took her leave. As she hurried up to her bedchamber under the eaves to stow the girdle away in her clothes chest, she realized how much the sensitive embroideress must be suffering in her anxiety for Eleanor. Keeping the secret that the little girl was still alive was proving harder than Gwyneth had ever imagined.

Gwyneth was in a fever of impatience to begin searching for the truth about Eleanor's disappearance, but Idony Mason kept her and her brother busy helping in the kitchen at the Crown for most of that day. The afternoon was well advanced before Gwyneth and Hereward had the chance to go out, and then only because Gwyneth explained that Ursus the hermit had promised her some healing herbs.

'Go then, and welcome,' said Idony, wrapping a loaf and the best part of a cold duck in a linen cloth. 'Take him that as a gift but mind you're back in time to help me serve supper.'

'Yes, mother.' Gwyneth took the bundle and hurried out into the street after Hereward.

The village was almost deserted. Gwyneth guessed that many of the villagers would still be looking for Eleanor. Even Rhys Freeman's shop was closed, suggesting that he too had joined the hunt.

'It would be so much easier if we could question Bedwyn,' she said to Hereward as they headed for the Tor. 'He can nod and shake his head, so if we thought of the right questions . . .'

Hereward was as practical as always. 'Master Thorson won't let us anywhere near Bedwyn.'

'Then maybe Ivo and Amabel could get in to see him.' Gwyneth refused to be put off. 'We could tell them what to say.'

'Maybe,' Hereward agreed cautiously. 'But Master Thorson has probably questioned him already.'

'Master Thorson believes he's guilty, just like everybody else,' Gwyneth retorted. 'Because of the necklace, and because he worked late that night. But plenty of other people work late.'

'And if Bedwyn knew the necklace was Eleanor's, he would never have given it to you,' Hereward added.

Gwyneth let out an exasperated sigh. 'People can be so *stupid*.'

She fell silent as they reached the edge of the village and had to concentrate on finding the right path through the marshes. Apart from questioning Bedwyn, there was no obvious way to make any progress. According to Hereward, the letter had given no indication of who had sent it. She was still worrying at the problem when they came to the river and she caught sight of Ursus sitting on a fallen log. Hurrying towards him, she held out the parcel of food.

'Good morrow, Ursus,' she said. 'Mother sent this.'

'Then give her my gracious thanks,' said the hermit, bowing his head. 'I am glad to have seen you today.' He handed Gwyneth a packet of herbs wrapped in cloth. 'These are for Edmund Hardwycke. His nursemaid should infuse them in water and give them to him to drink each morning. And these—' he handed her a smaller packet—'are for the guest at your inn. She should sprinkle them in a bowl of hot water and breathe in the steam.'

'Thank you,' said Gwyneth.

'And Bedwyn?' Ursus turned his brilliant blue eyes on her in a penetrating gaze. 'What news of him?'

Gwyneth exchanged a look with Hereward. Although she knew they ought to keep Lord Ralph's letter a secret, there could surely be no harm in telling Ursus? He talked so rarely, and she trusted him to understand the danger to Eleanor.

To her relief, Hereward caught her eye and nodded. He launched into an explanation about the letter, and how Father Godfrey believed that it was all a plot of Henry of Truro to finance his bid for the crown.

'And the letter asked for the abbey fish tank?' Ursus asked when Hereward had finished his story. 'That is a strange ransom indeed!'

Gwyneth realized the hermit was right. In the excitement of the previous evening when she had discovered that Eleanor was alive, she had hardly thought about the terms of the ransom. Now she wondered why Henry of Truro needed the precise amount of money that would fit into a cauldron.

'I saw the tank when I went to fetch the cloves for mother,' said Hereward. 'It's a huge iron cauldron. It will need a lot of gold to fill it. And that's strange, too,' he went on, sounding puzzled. 'The fish tank must be heavy enough when it's empty. When it's full of gold, no one will be able to lift it. Lord Ralph will have to take it to the meeting place separately, and fill it with gold when he gets it there. Why not just ask for a cartload of gold?'

'Why not?' Ursus said thoughtfully. 'A cauldron, you say . . .'

'Is there anything special about it?' Gwyneth asked. She was annoyed to think that she had never seen the fish tank for herself; being a girl, she was not allowed into the abbey kitchens. 'It's not made of gold, is it?'

Hereward raised his eyebrows. 'No, it's just a very big iron pot. And it has a crest on the side.'

'What kind of a crest?' Ursus's voice was suddenly sharp.

Hereward picked up a stick and began to sketch in the mud of the river bank. 'Something like this, I think.'

Gwyneth watched closely as the tip of her brother's stick traced outspread wings and a head with a pointed beak.

'A raven,' Ursus whispered. 'Hereward, that is the crest of Bran the Blessed.'

'Bran the Blessed?' Hereward echoed. 'Who's he?'

'He was an ancient warlord of the old people of Britain,' said Ursus.

A shout interrupted him, and the sound of two pairs of feet squelching rapidly through the marshes. A girl's voice called, 'Ivo, be careful with that net! Stop poking me with it!'

Hereward and Gwyneth turned towards the voices, and saw Ivo and Amabel Thorson emerge from the bushes. Ivo was carrying a fishing net on the end of a long pole, slashing at his twin with it as if it was a sword. When they reached the bank of the river, Amabel scooped up a handful of mud and hurled it at him.

Gwyneth sighed. 'It's all right, it's only—' she began, and broke off.

The log where Ursus had been sitting was empty. The hermit had vanished.

Chapter Nine

'The bones of King Arthur and his queen!' The young pilgrim leant over the table at the Crown and spoke earnestly to his companion. 'Never did I think to see such a wonder.'

'Aye.' His companion, an older man, took a mouthful of ale from his pewter mug and set it back on the table. 'Thank you, young mistress,' he said as Gwyneth bent over and refilled the mug from the pitcher she carried.

Gwyneth smiled and went to the barrel at the far end of the taproom to refill her jug.

Her father took the pitcher from her. 'I'll do that, Gwyneth. Your mother wants you in the kitchen.'

She hurried through the door. The two pilgrims she had just served were the last of the crowd who had filled the inn only a day or two before. Unless the truth about Eleanor was discovered soon, the village would sink back into poverty.

In the kitchen, Hereward had just removed the spit from the fire, and was helping his mother to set roast geese on serving platters.

'Gwyneth, help Hereward with this,' Idony said. 'I must make buttered eggs for Mistress le Fevre.'

She went out to the scullery where eggs and milk were set to keep cool. Gwyneth went over to the big central table and held a platter for the goose which Hereward was sliding off the spit. 'Have you thought any more about Bran the Blessed?' she asked him quietly.

Her brother shook his head. 'I could thump Ivo and Amabel for interrupting just then,' he said. 'Ursus was about to tell us about Bran and his cauldron.'

'Yes. It's as if he vanishes whenever other people come, but I wonder why?'

Hereward shrugged. 'If he wanted company, he wouldn't be a hermit. We'll have to go and look for him again if we want to find out about Bran the Blessed.'

'Bran the Blessed?' Idony Mason had returned, and paused in the doorway to the scullery with the bowl of eggs in her hand. Her cheeks were flushed from the heat of the kitchen and a strand of hair was escaping from its knot. 'My grandmother used to tell me tales of him.'

'What tales?' Gwyneth swung round eagerly, almost letting one of the geese slide to the floor in her haste.

'All kinds,' Idony said, smiling as she remembered. 'Bran was a giant of a man, so big that no house could contain him, and he once waded across the sea to Ireland to fight his enemies!'

Gwyneth and Hereward looked at each other. 'I . . . I don't suppose any of those tales mentioned a cauldron, did they?' Gwyneth ventured.

'A cauldron? But of course!' Idony exclaimed. 'There's not a soul alive who hasn't heard of Bran the Blessed's cauldron.'

'Well, we haven't,' said Hereward with exaggerated patience.

Gwyneth shot him a warning glance. 'Tell us, please, mother. It sounds fascinating.'

'Very well, but finish your task. Your father will want to carve those geese in a little while.' Idony brought the eggs to the table and began to crack them into a basin. 'Well now, where shall I begin? Bran's cauldron was huge and magical. According to the legends my grandmother told me, if a wounded warrior bathed in it, he would live for ever!'

'Then why aren't Bran's warriors still here today?' Hereward asked practically.

'There was a price to pay,' Idony explained. 'There's always a price for magic. The warrior would live for ever, but he would never be able to speak again. Not many of Bran's men would buy life so dearly, or so my grandmother always said.'

Gwyneth felt her heart miss a beat. Perhaps the abbey fish tank really was the magic cauldron! As her mother took the eggs to the fire, she leant over to Hereward and whispered excitedly, 'A cauldron like that would be very useful for Henry of Truro. If his men were injured, he could restore them. He wouldn't care that they would never speak again, so long as he could keep them to fight for him.'

Hereward nodded, his eyes huge. 'Perhaps the cauldron is the important part of the ransom, and not the gold at all.'

'And it's hidden away in the abbey kitchens!' Gwyneth grinned. 'I wonder what happens when they take the fish out? The brothers would get a shock if they leapt out of the pan and refused to be cooked!'

'The cauldron must only work for people,' Hereward decided. 'We need to discover who would know about it.' He tugged the last goose from the spit while Gwyneth held the platter to receive it. 'How did the man who sent the ransom note find out?'

'Well, the monks must have seen it many times, but they're holy men,' Gwyneth said. 'Even if they know the stories about Bran the Blessed, they probably don't believe them. They wouldn't have the cauldron in their kitchen if they did.'

At last they had found the end of the thread that might take them to the truth of what had happened to Eleanor. Whoever sent the ransom letter must have known about the abbey fish tank, and there couldn't be many people other than the monks who had seen it.

'Besides, the cauldron has been in the abbey kitchens for years and years, and yet it's only now that anyone has shown any interest in it. Someone must have seen it for the first time just lately.'

'We'll have to find out who,' said Hereward.

'You'll have to do that,' Gwyneth told him, with the familiar feeling of frustration that she wasn't allowed to go into the kitchen and question the monks herself. 'You can ask Brother Milo.'

'I'll do it tomorrow,' said Hereward resignedly. 'For Bedwyn's sake. I only hope Brother Milo doesn't throw a pot at my head!'

Early the next morning Hereward and Gwyneth brought breakfast from the Crown to the stone-masons on the building site. As soon as the monks emerged from prime Hereward hurried away to the kitchens.

He hesitated by the door as some of the younger monks appeared and took their places at the long tables down the centre of the room, ready to begin their tasks of chopping herbs and grinding spices in preparation for the brothers' mid-day meal. He was still trying to work out what to say; Gwyneth had a quicker tongue, and would have made a much better job of questioning Brother Milo.

Although it was still early, pots were already bubbling on the fire. At the far end of the room, in the shadows, stood the cauldron. Hereward peered at it, trying to make out the raven crest at this distance. He imagined a wounded warrior bathing in it and stepping out miraculously cured, but doomed never to speak again for all eternity.

Hereward wondered, if he knew he was dying, what choice he would make.

'Well, boy?' A sharp voice startled him out of his reverie. 'Why are you hovering around, getting under my feet?'

Hereward spun round to see Brother Milo glaring down at him. The refectioner was a short man with wiry dark hair around his tonsure and eyebrows like hairy caterpillars. His rope girdle stretched around a comfortable stomach, but the look he was giving Hereward was anything but a comfortable one.

Hereward realized he should have found himself an excuse for coming to the kitchens. He thought briefly of asking to borrow more spices, but to come again so soon would rouse Brother Milo's suspicions, when Idony Mason was usually so efficient. 'Your pardon, Brother,' he began awkwardly. 'I wanted to ask you—'

'Well, come in, come in. Don't stand there, you make the place look untidy.' Brother Milo strode over to the fire, grabbed a ladle, and tasted something from one of the pots. 'Brother Simeon!' he bellowed. 'Not enough salt, may God forgive you!'

The young novice scurried up with a box of salt and added some, pinch by pinch, while

Brother Milo tasted. At last the refectioner nodded. 'That's well. Go and fetch me rosemary leaves—fresh-picked, mind.'

Brother Simeon looked relieved to escape out into the herb garden, and Brother Milo turned back to Hereward. 'Well, boy, what is it?'

'If you please, Brother, it's about the fish tank.'

'The fish tank!' Brother Milo flourished the ladle and Hereward flinched, stepping backwards until his legs struck against a wooden pail. 'Not someone else who wants to steal my fish tank! Lord Ralph FitzStephen tells me,' Brother Milo went on, 'that my fish tank is not fitting for a great abbey such as this. A makeshift, he tells me. He will see to it that I have one more suitable, built of stone, and he will dispose of the old one for me.' He snorted. 'King's steward or no king's steward, what does he know of the matter? This fish tank has been good enough for the monks of Glastonbury for many a long year—since the time of the blessed Patrick, I'll warrant!'

He marched down the length of the kitchen to the cauldron and fetched it a ringing blow on the side with the ladle. 'That's good solid iron,' he announced. 'There's years of wear left in it.'

Hereward followed him and reached out to touch the cauldron, tracing the line of the raven's wing with one finger. 'Has anyone else except Lord Ralph been to look at the cauldron?' he asked.

Brother Milo gave him a sharp look but answered readily enough, his boiling anger reducing to a simmer. 'Strange you should ask that, boy. A few days ago, just before Lord Ralph's daughter went missing, that visiting lord was here. I brewed a posset to help his son sleep, and he came to fetch it. He had his eye on my cauldron, too!'

'Truly?' Hereward felt his stomach lurch with excitement.

'Aye. He stood there staring at it as if he'd never seen a cauldron before. Then he asked if he might have it—said the one he had in his kitchen wasn't big enough, and he would arrange for the abbey to have a new one.' Brother Milo sighed and raised his eyes to the ceiling. 'Well, Holy Scripture tells us to suffer fools gladly, so I told him with all courtesy that he must find his own fish tank. It's not my place to give away the abbey's goods. And now I'm going to lose it after all!'

'That's a great pity, sir,' Hereward said, trying to sound sympathetic while inwardly he was itching to get away and share this revelation with Gwyneth.

'So it is, boy. And what do *you* want?' he added to one of the young monks who had approached him holding out a bowl of chopped greens.

'These are ready for the soup, Brother,' said the young monk.

Grabbing the bowl, Brother Milo made his way back to the fire. 'Well, have you any more time-wasting questions?' he added to Hereward.

'No, sir, thank you.' Hereward backed hastily out of the kitchen, watching the iron fish tank fade into the shadows once more. He could hardly wait to tell Gwyneth that it was Lord Robert Hardwycke who had coveted the cauldron!

Gwyneth paced impatiently back and forth outside the half-built church. She wondered if Hereward would ask the right questions, or whether shyness would strike him dumb when faced with the formidable Brother Milo.

Suddenly, a voice spoke behind her. 'Lost your brother, Gwyneth?'

Starting, she turned to see Matt Green. 'No, master,' she replied. 'He has to go to the abbey kitchens.'

'I'm going that way myself,' said Master Green, flourishing a measuring rod. 'Lord Ralph wants me to measure up for a new fish tank—as if we hadn't enough to do, what with the fresh stone arriving and the search for that poor little maid.'

Lord Ralph must be getting the ransom ready, Gwyneth thought, so that he could go to the meeting place on the following evening. Things were moving fast, and the time they had to prove Bedwyn's innocence was running out.

'If I see Hereward I'll tell him to hurry,' Matt Green promised. He gave her a friendly nod as he walked towards the kitchens.

But there was no need for the stonemason to pass on the message. As he reached the door of the kitchens, Hereward burst out of it and came running across the grass to Gwyneth's side.

'Lord Robert!' he gasped, his face bright red with excitement. 'Lord Robert Hardwycke was asking about the cauldron. He must want it to heal Edmund!'

Gwyneth stared at her brother, who appeared to have lost his wits. 'What?'

'He visited the kitchens when he was here,' Hereward explained more slowly. 'He must have recognized the cauldron from the legend, because he asked if he could have it.'

'Then he really thinks it would make Edmund live for ever?' she murmured disbelievingly.

'He must do. But if he's right, then Edmund would never speak again.' Hereward's eyes stretched wide. 'And look what's happened to Bedwyn because he can't speak.'

'Lord Ralph must think that it's worth it, if the cauldron would save Edmund's life,' said Gwyneth. 'After all, he can hardly speak as it is.' She remembered the boy's quiet, rasping whisper, that seemed to exhaust his frail body.

Hereward nodded. 'It all makes sense. Lord Robert doesn't really want the gold at all. It's the cauldron that's important.'

'And he took Eleanor.' Anger stabbed through Gwyneth. 'How *could* he? With all his suffering from Edmund's illness, he must know what Lord Ralph is going through.'

'At least he won't hurt her,' said Hereward. 'He's not a murderous traitor like Henry of Truro. Lord Robert is a gentle man—you can see that by how much he cares about Edmund.'

126

That didn't excuse Lord Robert's behaviour in Gwyneth's eyes. 'Poor Eleanor! She must be so scared, all alone in a strange place. Listen, we've got to do something. If Lord Ralph takes the ransom to the meeting-place then he'll get Eleanor back, but they still might hang Bedwyn as a traitor. Lord Robert doesn't know that an innocent man has been arrested for his villainy.' She sat down on one of the blocks of dressed stone that lay waiting for the workmen, and tucked her skirt around her ankles. 'I suppose we could tell Father Godfrey,' she suggested uncertainly.

'Oh, of course.' Hereward sounded scornful. '"Please, Father Godfrey, this is a magic cauldron, and Lord Robert Hardwycke wants it so he can make Edmund live for ever." Can you not imagine what he would say?'

Gwyneth knew that her brother was right. Father Godfrey was a priest; he might believe in God-given miracles, but not in an ancient legend like the cauldron of Bran the Blessed. 'That's true,' she admitted. 'Besides, we can't be absolutely certain that Lord Robert did take Eleanor. Suppose we accused him, and then found out he didn't? We would be in so much trouble!'

Sighing, she stared up at her brother. 'What shall we do?'

Hereward frowned as if he was deep in thought. 'There is one way,' he said at last. 'But I don't see how we're going to manage it.' Gwyneth made an impatient noise before he slipped back into his reverie.

'We need to go to Lord Robert's castle,' Hereward announced. 'If Eleanor is there, we must set her free ourselves.'

Chapter Ten

'Yes!' Gwyneth sprang to her feet, eager to begin right away, and then paused. 'Lord Robert's estates are on the other side of Wells,' she said. 'However are we going to get there?'

Hereward shrugged. The only way to be sure they were right, and to save Bedwyn, was to search Lord Robert's castle to see if Eleanor was there. But that was so far away, the little girl might as well have been on the moon.

'There's not much time,' Gwyneth added. 'Lord Ralph has to take the ransom to the meeting place at dusk tomorrow.'

'Ursus said that everything has a time to be found,' said Hereward. 'Maybe, if we're meant to find Eleanor, there will be a way.'

'It had better be soon,' Gwyneth said impatiently. 'For Bedwyn's sake, and so the pilgrims feel safe to come to Glastonbury. Come on, let's take the herbs Ursus gave us to Brother Padraig.'

Hereward agreed, and fell in beside her as she headed for the infirmary. Gwyneth knew that she wouldn't be allowed to go inside to search for Brother Padraig, but before they reached the door she spotted the infirmarian in the herb garden on the far side of the kitchens. She waved, and hurried over to him.

'Well,' Brother Padraig said, straightening up from the herb bed and brushing soil from his hands. 'What can I do for you?'

'We've brought these herbs,' Gwyneth explained, fishing them out of the pouch at her belt. 'Ursus gave them to us for Edmund Hardwycke.'

'Do you remember the hermit who healed my ankle?' Hereward added.

'I do indeed,' Brother Padraig replied. 'One day I should like to meet him and discuss his remedies.' Taking the packet from Gwyneth, he opened it up, stirred the herbs inside with one finger and sniffed deeply. 'Juniper berries, leaves of mistletoe, root of dittany,' he murmured. 'Yes, all could be powerful against the falling sickness. Juniper and mistletoe I have used myself, but dittany is very hard to find. I have heard of its strength, but never had the chance to try it.' He wrapped up the package again. 'Abbot Henry has written some special prayers for Edmund and tomorrow Brother Timothy will take them to Lord Robert's castle and give them to his chaplain. He can carry these herbs with him, too.'

Gwyneth tensed and saw her own excitement reflected in Hereward's eyes. This could be the very stroke of luck that they needed, that one of the monks was going to make a special journey to Hardwycke so soon.

'Abbot Henry was deeply touched by Edmund's plight,' Brother Padraig went on. 'He will do all he can to aid him and his poor father.'

Gwyneth bit her lip to keep back an angry response. She had no pity at all for Lord Robert, who had stolen Eleanor and was keeping her far away from her father and everyone who loved her.

'Brother Padraig, may we go with Brother Timothy?' she asked instead. It was hard not to let her voice shake, she was so afraid that the monk would say no.

The infirmarian looked surprised. 'It's a long way, and—'

'Please!' Hereward begged. 'Edmund's our friend, and we'd love to see him again.'

'Mother and father can easily spare us from the inn for a day,' Gwyneth said. 'Almost all the pilgrims have left, so there isn't as much to do. We wouldn't be a nuisance to Brother Timothy,' she added.

Brother Padraig's eyes twinkled. 'I'm sure you wouldn't. Brother Timothy would enjoy your company, no doubt. And your friendship would be a God-given salve to that sick child.'

'Then we may go?' said Hereward.

'If your mother and father give you leave,' said Brother Padraig. 'Be outside the main gate tomorrow at the end of lauds. The way is long, so Brother Timothy will not wait for you.'

'Thank you! We won't be late,' Gwyneth assured him.

The infirmarian handed the herbs back to her. 'Then keep these, and I will tell Brother Timothy to expect you.'

Glancing at Hereward as they walked towards the abbey gate, Gwyneth saw that his eyes were shining. 'Ursus said there would be a way,' he said happily. 'And he was right.'

Dawn was seeping into the sky as Gwyneth and Hereward hurried along the street towards the abbey. The houses on either side were still quiet, their windows shuttered, their rooftops a black outline against the growing light.

Their mother and father had agreed to let them go with Brother Timothy. Idony Mason had been impressed by their concern for Edmund, and said that she felt sorry for the sick boy shut up in the castle with no other children to play with. Well, Gwyneth thought wryly, there was *one* other child in the castle, though Edmund probably had no idea that Eleanor was there.

Idony gave each of them a bag with bread and cheese and a waterskin for the journey. 'Mind you're polite to the holy brother,' she warned them as they left. 'And to Lord Robert, if you see him.'

As they approached the abbey, they saw Brother Timothy leading a mule cart through the gateway. Gwyneth waved and called a greeting, only to stop in dismay a moment later when a horseman followed Brother Timothy out of the gate.

There was no mistaking that superb black stallion, or the tall, haughty man in the saddle.

'It's Father Godfrey!' she whispered to Hereward. 'Why is he coming?'

Hereward shrugged, and then brightened. 'Maybe he's going home to Wells.'

The idea that they might be seeing the last of Godfrey de Massard allowed Gwyneth to greet the priest with a polite curtsy. She received a cool nod in return.

Brother Timothy's welcome was much warmer, though there was sadness in his eyes. Gwyneth guessed he was thinking of Eleanor, believing she would never be found.

'Good morrow, Gwyneth, Hereward. Climb up into the cart and let's be off. I've placed some sacks of straw there for you to sit on.'

Hereward scrambled up at once and Gwyneth followed, settling herself among the sacks as the cart jolted into motion.

'If we find Eleanor we can hide her under these sacks,' she whispered close to Hereward's ear. 'We'll be able to get her out of Hardwycke without anyone knowing.'

The creaking of the cart wheels and the clip-clop of the horse's hooves sounded loud in the early morning air as they made their way up the street and turned the corner onto the road to Wells. A few lights were beginning to show behind shutters, while here and there the smoke of house fires curled into the sky. There was no sign yet that the search for Eleanor had begun again;

Gwyneth feared that most people had given her up for dead.

There was enough daylight to show them the road ahead, a raised causeway over the marshy ground and scrubland that surrounded the village. Gwyneth suppressed a shiver of delight and drew her cloak closer. As much as she loved her home, it was exciting to go on a journey, especially with the prospect of finding Eleanor at the end it.

'Are you leaving Glastonbury, sir?' she asked, looking up at Father Godfrey.

The priest gave her a small, wintry smile. 'For a few hours only. I need to speak to Dean Alexander, but my duties in Glastonbury are not yet over. I shall return tonight.'

Gwyneth cast a disappointed glance at Hereward. It seemed that they were not to be rid of him after all!

'He must be going to report to the dean,' Hereward murmured when the priest had ridden a little way ahead.

The causeway led into dense woodland, where tree branches shut out the pale watery light. Father Godfrey's horse shied when a bird flew up from the side of the road but the priest expertly brought it under control.

Gwyneth hung over the side of the cart, looking for the track that led to the clearing with the old stone cross. That was where Lord Ralph was supposed to take the ransom. When she spotted it, she sat up and very nearly leant over to point it out to Hereward, then remembered that as far as Father Godfrey was concerned she knew nothing of the letter and the plans it contained.

By the time they emerged from the woodland the sun was well risen above the hills. The mists were clearing away and the sky had turned a pale, rain-washed blue. Ahead of them Gwyneth could see smoke drifting above the rooftops of a town, with the grey towers of Wells Cathedral rising above its walls.

The road led straight into the middle of the city. Gwyneth turned her head from side to side, trying to see everything at once. She had visited Wells twice before but she was still amazed at how big and crowded it was. The market-place was twice the size of the one in Glastonbury, full of people looking for bargains and street traders crying their wares. There were even tumblers, leaping and walking on their hands, something she had never seen in Glastonbury; Gwyneth craned her neck to get a better view as the cart trundled past. *Perhaps Glastonbury will be like this one day*, she thought longingly, as she saw the evidence of prosperity all around her.

The crowds spilled right across the street so that the mule cart had to slow down. The noise and bustle made Father Godfrey's horse nervous; it flung up its head, the bridle jingling, and baulked as he tried to ride it through the press of people.

'I'll bid you farewell from here,' he said. 'Carry my respects to Lord Robert, and my good wishes for his son's health.'

Brother Timothy raised a hand. 'I will, Father. And we'll look for you on the road home this evening.'

Gwyneth watched the priest steer his horse towards a gateway on the far side of the market-place. Through it she caught a glimpse of a stretch of green grass and the grey walls of the cathedral. A couple of plump, red-cheeked priests came out of the gateway and Father Godfrey paused to greet them.

Gradually the crowds thinned out and they left the last of the houses behind them. Now they were travelling through a very different land-scape with rich and well-kept farmland stretching on both sides of the road.

'We have reached Lord Robert Hardwycke's manor,' Brother Timothy told them.

'Is all this land his?' asked Hereward in surprise.

'Every foot of it.' Brother Timothy swept out an arm to take in all the countryside as far as they could see.

Gwyneth had not realized until then how wealthy Lord Robert must be. *And he still wants to take all Lord Ralph's gold!* she thought furiously, even more determined that he should have neither the gold nor the cauldron. Hereward had told her that Lord Ralph would be poor if he paid the ransom.

The fields they passed were divided neatly into strips, some bare and furrowed from recent ploughing, some left fallow and sporting a crop of weeds. Directly ahead of them, a rounded hill rose with a huddle of cottages around its base. On its summit loomed the grey stone walls of a castle. Banners flew from the battlements, in the scarlet and gold of Lord Robert's coat of arms.

Brother Timothy drove through the village and up the winding road that led to the castle. All round the walls was a steep-sided ditch, and across this stretched a drawbridge leading up to the main gate. Gwyneth felt suddenly daunted as she stared up at the vast stronghold.

The mule's hooves and the wheels of the cart sounded hollow on the wooden bridge. They halted in front of the gateway and Brother Timothy jumped down from the cart to tug at a bellrope. A deep-toned bell sounded in the gatehouse, and a moment later a porter appeared at one of the narrow windows.

'Who rides here to Hardwycke?' he demanded.

'Brother Timothy from Glastonbury Abbey,' the young monk replied. 'I have business with your chaplain, Father Paul.'

The porter vanished. There was a loud creaking sound and the portcullis began to slide upwards. With an encouraging grin at Gwyneth and Hereward, Brother Timothy climbed back onto the cart and took up the reins again. The gate was swung open, revealing men-at-arms on either side with sharp-pointed pikes in their hands.

The cart rolled forward into the shadows, under the lofty gateway of Hardwycke Castle.

Chapter Eleven

Brother Timothy brought the cart to a halt in the inner courtyard. At once a groom ran to the mule's head, and a servant appeared from the door of the massive keep. Bowing, he said, 'You're welcome, Brother. What may we do for you?'

'I come from Glastonbury,' Brother Timothy explained. 'I have a message for your chaplain, Father Paul. And these are friends of Edmund's from his stay in Glastonbury. They have come to visit him, and brought him healing herbs.'

The servant looked down his long nose at Gwyneth and Hereward. 'Master Edmund is resting after another fit,' he told them. 'It's highly unlikely that you will be allowed to see him. Lord Robert is very careful about whom he admits to his son's presence.'

Before Gwyneth could protest, the man bowed again. 'If you follow me, Brother, I will take you to Father Paul.'

Brother Timothy beckoned Gwyneth and Hereward to follow him. The servant led them inside the keep, down a short passage and through a door into a vast hall. Gwyneth let out a gasp. She had never seen such a magnificent room. Huge woven banners hung from roofbeams far above her head while tapestries decorated with pictures of hunting and battle covered the stone walls. In one tapestry a company of knights was riding in pursuit of a white stag, and it reminded Gwyneth of one of the tales of Arthur that her father had told her.

Hereward poked her in the ribs with his elbow. 'Stop gaping!'

Gwyneth realized that Brother Timothy was speaking to them. 'You had better stay here while I speak to Father Paul,' he said. Sounding embarrassed, he added, 'I'll see if he'll allow you to see Edmund and give him the herbs.'

He hurried after the servant who was waiting for him by a door at the far end of the hall.

As soon as they had gone, Gwyneth turned urgently to her brother. 'We'd better start looking for Eleanor,' she said. 'Before Brother Timothy comes back.'

'It could take days to search this place properly,' said Hereward, getting to his feet. 'Which way first?'

'Not through there, where Brother Timothy went,' Gwyneth decided. She walked over to a door about halfway down the hall and eased it open. It led into a smaller chamber hung with tapestries like the hall, furnished with a table and benches and two large chests against one wall. There were writing materials on the table, as if this was some kind of steward's room. At the far side was another door.

'There's no one here,' Gwyneth reported. 'Let's go this way.'

She felt hollow inside from a mixture of fear and excitement as she crept into the room with Hereward at her heels. 'I wonder where Lord Robert would put Eleanor?' she murmured.

'In the dungeons?' Hereward suggested.

'No. He loves Edmund, so I think he'd take better care of Eleanor than that,' Gwyneth decided. 'Perhaps in a bedchamber? We need to find a stair going upwards.'

She let out a cry of indignation when Hereward suddenly grabbed her and dragged her across the room into the window recess. At the same moment, the far door opened and she heard footsteps and voices. Shaking with fear, Gwyneth shrank back behind the edge of a tapestry. She caught a glimpse of two servants crossing the room, wearing the green livery of foresters or huntsmen.

'I tell you that hawk will never fly to the lure,' one insisted as he strode past their hiding-place. ''Twas taken too late from the nest.' Both men went into the great hall, and their voices were cut off as the door closed behind them.

Gwyneth remembered how to breathe. Hereward moved out into the room again, glancing cautiously up and down. Then he took the lead, going out through the far door where the servants had come from.

To their surprise, they found themselves standing outside on the edge of a garden, bounded on all sides by the grey walls of the castle. Narrow paths wound across lawns and through clumps of shrubs. In the summer it would be beautiful, Gwyneth guessed, but now it was all grey and cold.

Hereward was already creeping along beside the wall, peering into each window.

'I don't like this,' Gwyneth whispered, catching

him up. 'Anyone looking out will see us. Let's get inside again.'

The first door they came to was locked; Gwyneth felt her heart pound as Hereward struggled with the iron ring, imagining hostile eyes peering down at them from all the castle windows. She sped onwards, beckoning to her brother as she came to a second door.

To her relief, this one opened into a narrow hallway at the bottom of a spiral stair. Hereward peered upwards, his head cocked to listen. 'If anyone comes down we'll be caught for certain,' he murmured.

'That can't be helped. Go on!' Gwyneth urged him.

She followed closely as he began to climb, treading lightly so they could listen for the sounds of movement from above and below. At the top of the stairs they found themselves in a large chamber, bare except for benches round the walls and with a door on the opposite side, half open. Gwyneth bit back a gasp of terror when she saw a servant standing beside the fireplace. He had his back to them, removing the burnt out torches from iron sconces on each side of the hearth and replacing them with fresh ones.

While the servant was bent over his basket, Hereward beckoned to Gwyneth, and brother and sister darted silently across the room, through the open door and out into a passage. They did not stop until they were safely around the next corner.

'That was close!' Hereward whispered. He sagged, panting, against the nearest door, and jumped when it swung inwards with a creak.

A frail voice inside the room called out, 'Who's there?'

Gwyneth froze and clutched at Hereward's arm. The voice was Edmund's!

'Who's there?' he repeated.

Gwyneth was in half a mind to keep silent and hide, but she was afraid that Edmund's calling out might alert some of his servants. Besides, he might be frightened by someone prowling outside his bedchamber. Taking a deep breath, she pushed open the door and stepped inside. Hereward reached out as if he was going to stop her, then followed her in.

The room was dim because the window shutters were closed and the only light came from a taper burning on a table near the bed. By its yellow gleam Gwyneth could see richly embroidered hangings and a bedcover of brown fur. Edmund lay on a mound of pillows, looking as if he was half buried in the softness of the bed, his pale face turned towards the door.

As Gwyneth and Hereward stepped into the circle of light, he raised his head, blinking in surprise. 'It's you!' he rasped. 'What are you doing here?'

'We came with Brother Timothy,' Hereward explained. 'He brought some prayers from Abbot Henry, and we brought some herbs for you.'

Gwyneth decided to say nothing about their search for Eleanor. She could not imagine that Lord Robert had told his son what he had done.

'I'm sorry I can't get up,' Edmund murmured. 'I had another fit this morning.'

'Yes, we know,' said Hereward. 'One of your servants told us. We weren't supposed to come up to see you.'

'I'm glad you did.' Feebly Edmund reached out a hand towards them.

Just then Gwyneth heard a footstep in the passage outside. Hereward had closed the door behind them, and now someone was fumbling with the latch. Gwyneth looked round wildly, but there was no other way out.

'Quick, hide!' Edmund ordered in a whisper.

Gwyneth dived under the bed. Hereward scrambled in beside her and the bed hangings settled back into their folds just as the door creaked open.

'Master Edmund, I heard you cry out,' said a woman's voice. 'Have you had an evil dream? Here, sit up and let me turn your pillows.'

Edmund said something, but his voice was too soft for Gwyneth to make out the words through the heavy bed hangings. Above her head, the bed lurched as the boy sat up. She heard a murmur of voices, and then Edmund again, speaking more clearly.

'I wish there were some other children to talk to. I'm sick of being alone and silent all the time.'

You'll be silent for ever, Gwyneth thought sadly, *if your father dips you in the cauldron!*

'I know, my dear,' said the woman. 'But you can't have visitors when you're so ill. Your father has ordered you to rest. Maybe when you're older . . .'

Her voice died away, and Gwyneth felt as if she could read the woman's thoughts. Unless some miraculous cure was found, Edmund wouldn't live to be much older.

It was hot and dark underneath the bed. Gwyneth started to wonder how long they would have to stay there. She could not see Hereward, but she could feel him lying next to her, and hear the regular whisper of his breathing. Then the bed creaked and shifted again.

'There you go,' said the woman. 'Lie down again, Master Edmund. I'll speak to Father Paul, and maybe when his guest has gone he'll come and read to you.'

Gwyneth listened to her footsteps crossing the room, and the door opening and closing.

'You can come out now,' said a tiny voice.

Gwyneth crawled thankfully out from beneath the hangings and struggled to her feet, brushing dust from her skirt. She felt sticky and dishevelled. Hereward, following her out, was no better; his chestnut hair stuck up in clumps and his tunic was streaked with dirt. Whoever cleaned Edmund's room should pay more attention to underneath the bed, Gwyneth thought.

Her brother let out a huge sigh of relief. 'Thanks, Edmund,' he said. 'We'd better be going now.'

'Yes, before Father Paul catches you,' Edmund

replied. He blinked. 'Maybe if you come again, I might be out of bed.'

'The herbs we've brought might make you better.' Gwyneth felt a pang of sympathy for the lonely little boy. 'Then you could come to Glastonbury again and see us.'

The light died from Edmund's eyes. 'Maybe,' he said.

'Wait and see,' Gwyneth said, hoping that her faith in Ursus wasn't misplaced.

Hereward opened the door a crack and peered out. 'All's quiet,' he reported. 'We should go.'

With a hasty goodbye to Edmund, Gwyneth slipped out after her brother into the passage. But the door to the bedchamber had scarcely closed behind them when footsteps sounded ahead.

The only escape, apart from being trapped in Edmund's room again, was down another spiral stairway. Gwyneth grabbed Hereward and stumbled down the first turn of the stair as several people passed unseen along the passage above their heads. Not daring to go back up, they descended the rest of the way and found themselves in a stone-flagged passage at ground level. A window looked onto another part of the garden.

'This is hopeless!' Hereward complained. 'We're almost back where we started. It would take us a week to search this place.'

'Well, we haven't got a week.' Frustrated, Gwyneth looked down the passage. A delicious odour of roasting meat drifted towards her. 'That must be the kitchen,' she said, pointing.

'Well, Eleanor won't be there.' Hereward sniffed in his turn. 'I wish we were, though. I left my bread and cheese in the mule cart.'

'So did I.' Gwyneth tried to stop thinking about how hungry she was. 'Let's try the other way, then.'

She broke off as a servant rounded the corner with a tray of food in his hands. There was no way to avoid him and Gwyneth braced herself for a spate of questions.

As he drew abreast of them the servant gave them a suspicious look.

'If you please, sir,' Hereward began, jumping in before the man could speak, 'have you seen our father? He told us to wait for him.'

'No. What do I know of your father?' the servant snapped. 'Don't waste my time, boy.'

Suddenly a voice called, 'You there—wait!'

Gwyneth's heart lurched when she saw a boy

of about her own age, swathed in an apron, hurrying down the passage towards them. She felt herself go limp with relief when she realized that the boy was hurrying after the first servant.

'This got sent down with the tray this morning,' he said when he caught up with the man. 'Take it back, will you? The little maid will be missing it.' He was holding out a doll with flaxen hair and a richly embroidered gown.

Gwyneth gasped as she recognized Eleanor FitzStephen's favourite plaything, Melusine. She pressed herself against the wall, terrified that her excitement would give them away. Glancing at Hereward, she saw that his eyes were shining, fixed on the doll. The boy put the doll on the tray and sped back to the kitchens, leaving the servant to go on his way.

'Follow him!' Hereward whispered.

Together they crept along behind the servant. Gwyneth prayed fervently that they would not meet anyone else and have to hide again.

But fortune was with them. The servant climbed another stair, round and round and up and up until Gwyneth decided they must be in one of the towers. Glancing out of a window she looked down, dizzyingly, into the courtyard.

At last the servant stepped through a doorway on the stairs and came to a halt outside a door where a guard was standing, wearing the scarlet and gold surcoat of Lord Robert's men-at-arms.

Gwyneth and Hereward stayed on the stairs and peered out cautiously.

'Open up, will you?' the servant demanded. He sounded as rude speaking to the guard as he had to Hereward earlier.

'All right, Martin, all right.' The guard unhooked a key from his belt. 'No need to be in such a taking.'

'You would be in a taking if you had to run around all day after a little wench who shouldn't be here in the first place. What Lord Robert is thinking of, I don't know! What next, I ask?'

While Martin was complaining, the guard unlocked the door and held it open. The servant went in and Gwyneth heard Eleanor's voice, crying out, 'Melusine!' as she recognized her doll.

'She's there!' Gwyneth whispered, giving Hereward an excited glance.

Martin came out of the room again almost at once and locked the door behind him. He stalked off without another word to the guard; Gwyneth and Hereward climbed a few steps higher to avoid him as he reached the stairway and disappeared down it.

'He's left the key in the lock,' Hereward pointed out, breathing the words into Gwyneth's ear. 'If only we could get rid of the guard, we'd be able to unlock the door.'

Gwyneth thought hard. They could go back to Brother Timothy, tell him what they had discovered and let him deal with it; but if Lord Robert knew that Eleanor had been found, he might be able to have her moved, so it would look as if Gwyneth and Hereward had been lying. Somehow, they had to get Eleanor out of Hardwycke before Lord Robert knew that she had gone.

Then an idea came to her. Turning to Hereward, she whispered, 'I'm going to distract the guard. When he's not looking, get the key.'

Without giving Hereward the chance to ask questions, she stepped out from the stairway and approached the guard.

'Well, young mistress,' said the man. He was about her father's age, and Gwyneth thought he had a kind face. 'I don't think I've seen you before.'

'No—' Gwyneth pretended to stumble on the corner of one of the flagstones and flung herself forward. The impact as she fell to the ground jarred her whole body. She closed her eyes as if momentarily stunned, and heard the guard's footsteps draw closer and Hereward's quicker ones speeding past her to the door.

'Young mistress?' Gwyneth felt the guard's hand on her shoulder. 'Are you hurt?'

Gwyneth let her eyes flutter open. 'Oh . . .' she groaned. 'I fell . . . how stupid . . .'

The guard crouched down beside her, and Hereward came to join him. 'Here, sit up,' he said with brotherly concern, putting an arm round Gwyneth. 'Mother always says she never looks where she's going,' he added to the guard.

Gwyneth was feeling shaken enough to appreciate the man's look of sympathy. She had fallen harder than she meant to, skinning her hands on the rough stone, and one of her knees stung. 'Thank you, sir,' she said. 'I'll be well if I sit for a moment.'

'You want to go to old Annet,' the guard said, examining her hands where beads of blood were welling through the scraped skin. 'She'll give you a salve for that.'

Gwyneth didn't know who old Annet was, but she had more sense than to ask, if she was supposed to be well known to all the people at Hardwycke.

The guard straightened up, leaving her sitting on the floor. 'Now, where's that key?' he exclaimed, staring at the empty keyhole. He slapped his belt, failed to find the key there, and swung round with a baffled look on his face.

'Maybe Martin took it with him?' Hereward suggested helpfully.

The guard muttered a curse under his breath. 'He's been a nuisance from the day he was born,' he said. Checking that the door was locked, he hurried off down the stairs, shouting, 'Martin! Martin!'

Once he had gone, Hereward produced the key from his tunic. Gwyneth got up, stifling a genuine groan. She limped over to the door as Hereward unlocked it with a worried glance over his shoulder. He pushed it open and Gwyneth followed him into the room.

The first thing she noticed was how pretty the chamber was. The walls were hung with tapestries, there was a bright fire in the hearth, and a bed with silken hangings embroidered with flowers. A cloth doll, a wooden top, and a cup and ball were piled with other toys on top of a silver-mounted chest against one wall. Clearly Lord Robert had done everything he could to make his little prisoner feel welcome.

Just as clearly, his efforts had not worked. The toys did not look as if they had been played with, and Eleanor was curled up in the window seat with her arms round Melusine. She looked up fearfully, her face pale and streaked with tears, as Hereward and Gwyneth came into the room.

'Hello, Eleanor,' said Gwyneth. 'Do you remember us?'

For a moment the little girl looked bewildered. Then her eyes widened. 'Gwyneth? Hereward?'

'That's right,' said Hereward. 'We've come to take you home.'

Eleanor sprang up and flung herself at them, burying her face in Gwyneth's shoulder.

Gwyneth could feel that she was shaking. 'Hush now,' she said. 'Eleanor, don't cry.'

The little girl looked up. She wasn't crying, although her mouth was trembling. 'Is father here?'

'No, he doesn't know where you are. He's been frantic with worry for you.'

'But he said I could come!'

'Who told you that?' said Hereward, frowning.

'Lord Robert. He said I would be able to play with Edmund and cheer him up, but I haven't seen him at all. Is he poorly again?'

Gwyneth glanced at Hereward. 'Yes, he's not well enough to play,' she told Eleanor. 'We've got to go now, before that guard comes back.'

Grasping Eleanor's hand, she pulled the little girl out of the room. Hereward closed the door behind them, locked it, and took the key with him. 'That might slow them down,' he said.

All was quiet on the stairs. Presumably the guard was still looking for Martin. Hereward took the lead and they hurried down. Gwyneth had seen that the tower opened onto the main court-yard; with luck, they would be able to hide Eleanor among the sacks on the mule cart until they were safely away from Hardwycke.

They reached the bottom of the stairs without meeting anyone. The door to the courtyard was straight in front of them. Hereward glanced swiftly up and down the passage and beckoned to Gwyneth and Eleanor. 'It's safe, come on.'

But as they darted across the passage the door swung open. Gwyneth bit back a cry when she saw who stood there looking down at them.

It was Lord Robert Hardwycke.

Chapter Twelve

For a moment Lord Robert did not move. Shock, guilt, and confusion battled in his face. *What would he do now?* Gwyneth wondered frantically. *Would he take them all prisoner?*

Taking a deep breath, she stepped forward. 'Lord Robert, we know about the cauldron.'

The nobleman flinched as if he had been struck and put a hand out to steady himself against the doorpost. 'You know?' With a desperate effort to recover himself he added more harshly, 'What do you know?'

'We know that the abbey fish tank is the cauldron of Bran the Blessed,' replied Hereward, coming to stand beside his sister. 'You took Eleanor so that Lord Ralph would have to give it to you.'

Lord Robert squeezed his eyes shut and let out a low groan. 'I did it for Edmund. I did it to save my son.'

'But it won't save him!' Gwyneth ran up to the stricken man and dared to lay a hand on his arm. 'Except for his illness, Edmund is an ordinary boy. If you dip him in the cauldron, he'll never speak again. He'll never be able to have friends, or live a normal life, for ever and ever. Is that what you want for him?' When Lord Robert did not reply, she added, 'Have you asked Edmund if that's what *he* wants?'

Lord Robert's eyes met hers, and she saw all his grief there. 'But he's my son, my only son,' he whispered. 'My heart will not sustain me to see him die.'

'He needn't die.' Gwyneth reached into her pouch and took out the packet of herbs Ursus had given her. 'These herbs came from a hermit on the Tor,' she told him, pushing the packet into his hands. 'If you infuse a little in water and let Edmund drink it each morning, he will become stronger. He might even get better,' she added, willing Lord Robert to believe her.

For a long moment he stood in silence, gazing down at the cloth-wrapped packet. Gwyneth saw tears on his face.

'Yet with the cauldron I would be sure he would live,' he said.

'But what would he live *for*?' Gwyneth cast an anguished glance at her brother.

'We haven't met Edmund many times, but we like him already,' Hereward began, frowning in his effort to find the right words. 'He's brave and friendly, and there are things in life he can enjoy. How would he ever enjoy life again if he couldn't speak?'

Lord Robert gazed at him, and then at Gwyneth, for what seemed like an eternity. At last he stepped aside. 'Go,' he said.

Weak with relief, Gwyneth curtsied to him and took Eleanor's hand to lead her out into the courtyard. As they walked past him, Lord Robert stooped down to Eleanor and laid his hand on her hair. Eleanor looked up with uncertainty in her blue eyes.

'You're a good girl,' he murmured. 'Forgive me.'

Eleanor stared reproachfully at him. 'You said my father gave me leave to come and stay.'

'I'm sorry.' Lord Robert's voice was shaking. 'I thought it was the only way.'

Hastily he wiped his face and strode out into the courtyard, calling for Brother Timothy's mule cart to be harnessed. At the same moment, Brother Timothy appeared from the main door to the keep and hurried over to Gwyneth and Hereward.

'Where have you been?' he asked, sounding annoyed. 'Father Paul and I have been looking everywhere.' He fell silent as his astonished gaze landed on Eleanor.

'We'll tell you all about it on the way,' Gwyneth promised. 'Everything is all right now.'

Brother Timothy looked doubtful, but Lord Robert was already withdrawing into the keep without waiting to say a proper farewell. Gwyneth felt a pang of pity for him, and she prayed that Ursus's herbs would help Edmund recover his strength.

The mule cart was brought up, and the portcullis raised. Gwyneth helped Eleanor into the cart but Brother Timothy was still staring after Lord Robert, his face full of questions.

'Trust me!' she said urgently. 'We must go, in case he changes his mind.'

Brother Timothy gave her a bewildered look but he took his seat at the front of the cart and gathered up the reins. Gwyneth and Hereward scrambled up beside Eleanor, and Brother Timothy drove them out through the gates and down the hill.

Eleanor bounced happily on the sacks of straw, earnestly telling Melusine that they would be home soon.

Hereward shared out the bread and cheese. 'How did Lord Robert take you away from Glastonbury?' he asked as he handed some to Eleanor.

The little girl's eyes grew huge with remembering. 'I promised Edmund I would take him to see Arthur's bones,' she began. 'I got up really early, before Hilde was awake. Edmund and his father and I went into the chapel.' Her face grew shadowed. 'But then Edmund fell down and cried out as if something was hurting him. He went limp and at first I thought he was dead. His father started to cry. I wanted to fetch father, but Lord Robert said Edmund would get better if I came to Hardwycke to keep him company for a while.'

'What happened next?' Gwyneth prompted.

'Lord Robert carried Edmund to his litter, and he said I should travel in the cart with the cushions and hangings. He said it would be warm and comfortable, but I wanted to see where we were going. I put my head out, and one of the guards shouted at me to get back.' She looked sad as she added, 'He made me jump and I lost my pretty necklace.'

Gwyneth shot an excited glance at Hereward. 'Then that's how Bedwyn found it!' she exclaimed. 'Eleanor dropped the necklace in the woods, and he must have picked it up.'

'So Bedwyn is innocent!' said Brother Timothy, turning round from his seat on the front of the cart. 'God be praised. I never wished to think that man would harm a child.'

By the time they had passed through the city of Wells the daylight was beginning to fade. Eleanor had curled up among the sacks of straw and gone to sleep. Somewhere far ahead, Gwyneth caught sight of a glint of flame, bobbing amid the trees. It grew larger as they drove along, and Gwyneth saw that it was moving. At last, drawing closer still, she made out a couple of carts pulled by oxen, escorted by men on horseback with blazing torches in their hands.

The first cart was piled with fat canvas bags filled with something that gave the unmistakable chink of gold when one of the wheels jolted against a stone. In the second was a huge black cauldron, the fish tank from Glastonbury Abbey that had once revived the wounded warriors of

Bran the Blessed. Gwyneth could just make out the raven crest; the widespread wings seemed to beat in the flickering light of the torches as if the bird might tear itself free from the confining iron and flap away into the sky.

Now she was close enough to see that the cloaked and hooded man driving the first cart was Lord Ralph FitzStephen. She tugged at Eleanor's shoulder. 'Eleanor, wake up! Your father's here!'

The little girl sat up, blinking. Lord Ralph halted his mule and stared as if he could not believe what he was seeing. 'Eleanor?' he said hoarsely.

'Father!' Eleanor squealed with excitement and jumped down from the cart.

Lord Ralph pulled her up beside him and held her close with his face hidden in her hair. After a few moments he looked up and peered through the twilight to see who had brought his daughter back to him. 'Brother Timothy, is that you? And Gwyneth, and Hereward? Will someone tell me what is going on?'

'We found your daughter at Hardwycke, my lord,' Brother Timothy replied.

'At Hardwycke?' Lord Ralph's voice was incredulous. 'What was she doing there?'

Gwyneth and Hereward slid down from the mule cart and walked forward until they reached Lord Ralph. Gwyneth glanced back at Brother Timothy, uncertain of how much she ought to tell the steward about Lord Robert's crime, and saw the young monk give her an encouraging nod.

'You have Eleanor back safely, my lord,' she said. 'Does it matter where she's been, or why?'

'Of course it matters!' Lord Ralph snapped. 'Tell me at once.'

'Lord Robert took her,' Gwyneth admitted. Knowing instinctively that she should not reveal the secret of the cauldron, she added, 'He thought her company would help Edmund. When he realized the error of what he had done, he thought to disguise his foolish crime by demanding the ransom. I'm sure he always intended to return her to you safely, my lord.'

'Lord Robert stole her?' Lord Ralph's mouth was a grim line. 'Then I'll ride to Hardwycke at once. He'll answer to my sword for what he's done to her.'

'Don't, my lord. Please don't!' Gwyneth begged, quite forgetting that she was daring to challenge a nobleman. 'Lord Robert isn't a bad man. He was mad with grief for his son.'

Lord Ralph narrowed his eyes thoughtfully.

'My lord, remember how you felt when Eleanor was lost,' Hereward put in. 'How would you feel if you knew that she was going to die?'

Lord Ralph let out a long sigh and settled Eleanor more comfortably in his arms. 'I know not why you plead for him, but how can I deny you, when you have brought my daughter back to me?' Straightening up, he turned to give an order to the driver of the second cart. 'Unyoke the oxen and push the cart off the road. No need to drag that lump of iron back to the abbey. There are stonemasons ready to build a new fish tank.'

Gwyneth stared in dismay as the driver jumped down and began to unfasten the harness. They couldn't abandon the cauldron of Bran the Blessed by the side of the road! Someone would find it and maybe discover its secret, and in the hands of wicked men like Henry of Truro it could do untold harm.

'Please, my lord,' Hereward said hastily. 'Let the holy brothers have their fish tank back. Brother Milo was grieved to lose it, and it will save the time and trouble of building a new one.'

'That's true,' Lord Ralph admitted to Gwyneth's

relief. 'Very well, take it back. The good Lord knows we don't have money to spare from the rebuilding.'

Suddenly there was the sound of hoofbeats coming from the direction of Wells, and a few moments later Godfrey de Massard rode into the circle of torchlight.

'Lord Ralph?' he began, and then exclaimed, startled, 'Eleanor! She's safe!' A rare smile lit up his face.

'Safe indeed,' Lord Ralph replied. 'All thanks to Brother Timothy and these children. They brought her back from Hardwycke.'

'Hardwycke? What was the child doing there?'

Lord Ralph hesitated. 'It was a misunderstanding,' he said at last. 'Let us thank God she is home safe.'

'Yes, indeed.' Father Godfrey's smile faded, and Gwyneth thought that he looked disappointed. 'So Henry of Truro had nothing to do with it?'

'No, he's innocent of this at least,' Lord Ralph said.

'And so is Bedwyn,' Gwyneth added daringly, going to stand beside Father Godfrey's horse and looking up at him. 'He didn't take Eleanor. Can he be freed now?'

Father Godfrey stared at her for a few moments, his eyes cold and hard. Then he gave a tiny nod. 'Very well. Lord Ralph, if I can do nothing for you here, I will ride at once to Finn Thorson and see that the stonemason is released.'

'Certainly, Father Godfrey, go at once.'

The priest set spurs to his horse and trotted off into the night. Gwyneth and Hereward shared a look of triumph. They had found Eleanor, and Bedwyn would go free!

Chapter Thirteen

'Mistress le Fevre, have you heard the news?' It was the following morning, and Gwyneth was taking a tray of wine and honey cakes to Marion's bedchamber. 'Bedwyn is free! Ivo and Amabel Thorson just came to tell us.'

Marion looked up from putting on her cloak, and Anne Mason turned from her work at the table. Since the night before, when Gwyneth and Hereward had brought the news back to the Crown of how they had discovered Eleanor safe at Hardwycke, Marion had already cut out the linen for the little girl's gown, and now Anne was tracing the pattern for the embroidery.

'God be thanked!' Marion said fervently, clasping her hands as if in prayer. More thoughtfully she added, 'Perhaps the stonemason will leave Glastonbury now. He will scarcely wish to stay in a place where he was suspected of murder.'

'I don't think so,' said Gwyneth. 'There's still work for him to do at the abbey. I expect he'll go back there.'

'Perhaps . . .' Marion's slender fingers went to the clasp of her cloak, but she paused before fastening it.

Gwyneth set the tray down on the table where her aunt was working. 'The gown will be beautiful,' she said, admiring the clear blue of the linen. 'Eleanor will love it.'

'Let us hope it helps her forget her ordeal,' said Aunt Anne. 'Poor child! And the whole village believing it was Bedwyn.' She shook her head and clicked her tongue disapprovingly, as if she had already forgotten that she had been one of Bedwyn's chief accusers.

'But all's well now,' Gwyneth said.

Marion nodded and went to look out of the window. 'The sky threatens rain,' she said. 'I need to match some thread at the market, but I fear catching a chill.'

'I can fetch it for you,' said Anne Mason.

'Thank you,' said Marion, slipping off her cloak and laying it back in its place. 'Perhaps tomorrow I shall feel well enough to venture out.'

Leaving the embroideress hunting for the

fabric she needed to match with the new thread, Gwyneth went downstairs.

Hereward was coming in from the yard. 'There you are!' he said. 'I've finished my tasks for father. Let's go and see if we can find Ursus. I can't wait to tell him about Bedwyn!'

Gwyneth hurried into the kitchen to fetch her cloak and make sure there were no more tasks to do.

'Of course you may go,' said Idony. 'But mind you're back in time to help with dinner.'

Gwyneth bid a hasty goodbye and ran into the yard where Hereward was waiting.

In the market-place, Bedwyn was buying a loaf of bread at the baker's stall. Several of the villagers shot uneasy glances at him as if they were not quite sure what to make of him, but no one spoke to him with hostility or refused to serve him. Gwyneth saw a gleam of satisfaction in Hereward's eyes. She grinned, sharing his triumph that they had helped to prove Bedwyn's innocence.

Her delight swelled when she saw Mistress Flax bustle up to the stonemason and heard her say, 'Your pardon, Master Bedwyn, for what we thought of you. You're welcome in the village now.'

Bedwyn gave her a courtly bow, but his face turned dusky red with embarrassment and he did not meet the weaver's eyes.

Tom Smith rested a hand on Mistress Flax's shoulder. 'Best leave him alone, mistress,' he advised. 'Let him forget the danger he was in, and all the chatter of evil tongues.'

'But—' Mistress Flax began to protest, only to break off as Bedwyn turned away and strode quickly in the direction of the abbey.

'Tom Smith is right,' Hereward agreed quietly to Gwyneth. 'Bedwyn won't want a fuss.'

A cold spatter of rain began to fall as they followed the winding paths through the marshes. To Gwyneth's surprise, they found the hermit quite quickly among the thorn trees at the foot of the Tor, with a bundle of firewood on one shoulder.

'Good morrow,' he said. 'I see by your faces you have news. Is it about the stonemason?'

Setting down his bundle, he squatted on the ground and listened while Gwyneth and Hereward poured out the tale.

'You were right!' Hereward exclaimed. 'The abbey fish tank is the cauldron of Bran the Blessed. Lord Robert Hardwycke wanted to dip Edmund into it, to cure him of the falling sickness.'

'That's why he stole Eleanor FitzStephen,' Gwyneth continued. 'So that Lord Ralph would give him the cauldron.'

Ursus nodded as if he was confirming something in his own mind. 'But Eleanor is home now?'

'Yes, all is well now,' Gwyneth replied.

'And Brother Milo has his fish tank back,' Hereward added.

'The abbey kitchen is much the best place for it,' said Gwyneth. 'We're sorry for Lord Robert, but Edmund is much better off without it.'

'You show more wisdom than his father.' Ursus's piercing blue eyes rested on Gwyneth for a moment. 'The power that the cauldron holds is dangerous for ordinary men. And Bedwyn?' he pressed. 'Is he set free?'

'Oh yes,' Hereward replied. 'He's back at work at the abbey.'

'Then there is something you can do for me,' Ursus told them.

'What is it?' asked Gwyneth.

'Bring Bedwyn to me.'

Gwyneth stared at the hermit in surprise. 'Here, now? What if he won't come?'

'I think he will.' Ursus was still serious, though a smile glinted in his eyes.

'We'll try,' Hereward said uncertainly. 'Will you wait for us?'

'I shall be here,' Ursus promised.

The silent man was hard at work when Gwyneth and Hereward reached the abbey grounds. He was smoothing the sides of a block of stone with hammer and chisel, making it ready for the craftsmen to set in place. He rose to his feet and bowed when he saw Hereward and Gwyneth, and his rare smile appeared.

'We're glad to see you free,' Hereward said. 'We've brought you a message.'

'Someone wants to see you,' explained Gwyneth. 'A hermit on the Tor. He wants you to come with us now.'

Bedwyn frowned and bent over his stone again, giving it a few more strokes with the chisel. Gwyneth wondered if that meant he would not come, but before she could think what to say the huge man drew one hand across the surface of the stone, his face solemn, and laid down his tools. Then he straightened up and gestured to Gwyneth and Hereward to lead the way.

The three of them hurried towards the abbey

gate. Owen Mason was deep in discussion with Matt Green over a stone carving, and the other masons were all hard at work. No one seemed to notice them go. Gwyneth was relieved; she would have found it hard to explain why Bedwyn was leaving his work in the middle of the day.

Hereward took the lead as they approached the Tor, heading for the thorn trees where they had left Ursus. The hermit was still there, just as he had promised, sitting on a fallen tree with his arms wrapped round his knees.

As the stonemason approached, Ursus rose and spread his hands wide. His blue eyes were alight with warmth and gentleness. 'Bedwyn. You are most welcome.'

Bedwyn drew closer until he stood in front of Ursus. His dark eyes searched the hermit's face. Then to Gwyneth's amazement he fell to his knees and covered his face with his hands. She looked at Hereward, who shrugged as if he was equally puzzled.

Ursus lightly touched his shoulder. 'Rise, my friend,' he said. 'Come.'

He turned along a narrow path that led upwards through the thorn bushes. Bedwyn got to his feet and began to follow like a man in a dream. Gwyneth and Hereward brought up the rear; Gwyneth was reminded of the time Ursus had shown them the tunnel under the Tor, where they had found the lost cross. She felt as though she was standing on the threshold of something wondrous, and did not know whether to be excited or afraid.

The path emerged from the thorn trees and Gwyneth saw that they were standing on the lower slopes of the Tor. Above them the hillside rose almost sheer towards the summit. Ursus paused to look back and said again, 'Come.'

He climbed the steep slope towards a huge slab of rock that was set in the side of the hill, and waited on a narrow ledge in front of the slab until Bedwyn stood by his side, and Gwyneth and Hereward had scrambled up after him. Bedwyn glanced at Ursus, who gave him a tiny nod. The stonemason began to scrape the moss away from the centre of the rock. Gwyneth watched in fascination as deeply gouged lines began to appear. She caught her breath when she realized that they formed the weathered outline of a dragon's head.

'What's happening?' she exclaimed, turning to Ursus. 'What is this place?'

A rumbling sound, loud as a clap of thunder, answered her. Spinning round, she saw that Bedwyn was pushing at the slab of rock. Corded muscles in his neck and arms stood out as he exerted all his strength and the massive stone slid to one side.

Behind it, a tunnel the height of a tall man stretched away, leading deep into the heart of the Tor.

Chapter Fourteen

Gwyneth and Hereward stared at the tunnel in disbelief. Hereward could not imagine why they had never noticed the slab of rock before, nor guessed that the Tor had yet more secrets to reveal.

The tunnel quickly became taller, so that even Bedwyn did not have to stoop when he stepped through the entrance. The floor was paved with flagstones and the walls and roof had been smoothed with a hundred skilful chisels. This was no accidental hole carved out by water, like the tunnel they had used to find the cross, but the work of many long-forgotten craftsmen.

Bedwyn walked forward a few paces and then turned, beckoning to Hereward and Gwyneth.

Hereward glanced questioningly at Ursus. The hermit smiled and gestured for them to enter. Hereward was certain that the tunnel held no mysteries for him.

Gwyneth had already stepped into the

entrance, where she stood looking back impatiently. 'Come on,' she said. 'We'll lose Bedwyn if you stand there dithering.'

Hereward hesitated a moment longer. 'Will you give us a taper to light the way?' he asked Ursus, remembering how the hermit had provided them with light to explore the first tunnel.

'You will not need it,' Ursus replied.

'Hereward, come on!' Gwyneth repeated.

Swallowing his nervousness, Hereward walked into the tunnel behind Bedwyn and his sister.

The passage led straight onwards, sloping gently down. As the light from the entrance died away behind them, Hereward realized why they did not need a taper. Torches set in iron brackets lined the tunnel walls, and as Bedwyn approached them they sprang into life, flickering with cold flame.

The passage gave way to a flight of shallow steps, and then led smoothly on again. Bedwyn paced forward without looking round to see if Hereward and Gwyneth were following. At last the passage ended in an archway, outlined against a brighter light beyond. Bedwyn passed through; after an instant's hesitation Hereward and Gwyneth followed.

The archway led into a vast cavern. Hereward stumbled to a halt, hearing his sister gasp with amazement. A ring of lanterns on iron stands were set around a stone table in the middle of the cave. Lying on it was a horn taken from some enormous animal, mounted with silver and carved with twisting patterns. Hereward wondered who it belonged to, or who would dare sound it.

As his eyes grew more accustomed to the light, he realized that the cavern held greater wonders still. The floor was sanded, and through the sand lines had been drawn to divide it into segments, all converging on the table. Around the cave walls, half-hidden in shadow, each segment held a sleeping knight. Their mail shimmered grey like water under a winter sky. Each man's hands were clasped around the hilt of his sword, which lay flat on his chest pointing to the centre of the circle. Behind each head, a shield rested against the wall, their bright blazons splashing colour against the grey rock.

'What is this place?' Gwyneth whispered.

'This is the Cavern of Sleeping Warriors,' replied a rough and unfamiliar voice.

Hereward jumped. Bedwyn had spoken! Spinning round, he saw the huge man standing a

185

little further round the circle. 'Bedwyn! I thought you couldn't speak,' he said.

'Out there, I could not.' Bedwyn cleared his throat. 'Black magic kept me silent through many a long year.'

'What happened? And who are you, sir?' Gwyneth stammered, her eyes huge.

'My name is Bedivere,' he said, 'and I am the last of the Knights of the Round Table. These men sleeping here—' he gestured to the figures around him—'are my fellow warriors, awaiting the signal to rise up and fight for Arthur's people once again.'

'But, sir, how is it that you are not sleeping with them?' Hereward asked. He could not stop staring at the stonemason. This man had actually spoken with King Arthur! He must be hundreds of years old—but how?

'I was tricked,' repeated Bedwyn—no, *Bedivere*, Hereward reminded himself. 'After Arthur's last battle, when he lay wounded to death, I cast his sword Excalibur into the lake, back to the hand that forged it, and I saw Arthur himself carried off to Avalon to be healed of his wounds.'

'Avalon? That's here, Glastonbury,' Gwyneth breathed.

'So they say.' Bedivere smiled at her and took up his story again. 'My own wounds were grievous, and when Arthur had gone I lay down to die. That was when she came to me—the witch queen, Morgan le Fay. She was Arthur's half-sister, and always she hated him and worked to do him harm. I was a fool to trust her. She told me that if I bathed in the cauldron of Bran the Blessed, my wounds would be healed.'

Gwyneth and Hereward exchanged startled looks. Here was someone struck dumb in order to live for ever, just as Lord Robert had wanted for his son! And a heavy price it had been, resulting in false imprisonment and loneliness.

'For once Morgan did not lie to me,' said Bedivere, 'though she hid part of the truth. My wounds were healed, but the power of speech was taken from me. I was doomed to live on, alone and friendless, always seeking the resting place of my brother warriors, for Morgan said that if I could find this cave, the enchantment would be lifted. She laughed when she told me, because she knew that my torment would be all the greater if one faint hope remained to me.'

'You sought the cave for so long . . .' Gwyneth whispered, her gaze fixed on Bedivere.

The knight bowed his head. 'And now that I have found it, I shall sleep with my comrades until the time comes for us to rise and fight once more at Arthur's side.'

He began to pace slowly around the circle, and Hereward saw his tears spill over as he gazed on the faces of the men who had been his friends.

'Kay . . . valiant heart,' he murmured. 'Do you dream of the days when we rode out together? And Gawain of the golden tongue . . . How I have yearned to take my place beside you!'

He paused for a moment beside an empty segment, where the shield at its head showed three golden crowns on a scarlet background. Bedivere bowed and passed on until he came to yet another empty place. Here was a shield displaying a golden pennant, and a sword lying on the sand.

Bedivere stooped and took up the sword, his hand closing easily around the hilt. He drew the blade through the air with a silken sound, and then reversed it and held it hilt uppermost in the form of a cross.

'I thank you with all my heart,' he said, looking at Hereward and Gwyneth. 'You have saved me from a curse more grievous than any wound dealt in battle.'

A distant rumbling sounded, and sudden alarm flared in Bedivere's eyes. 'Run!' he shouted.

Bewildered, Hereward looked around. The cave was still peaceful; the sleeping knights had not stirred. Again Bedivere bellowed, 'Run!'

Gwyneth whipped round in a swirl of skirts. 'The stone is moving!' she gasped. 'We'll be trapped!'

In the same instant Hereward recognized the sound. The rock at the mouth of the tunnel was sliding back, about to entomb them for ever beneath the Tor. Hard on Gwyneth's heels he sped back to the entrance of the cave.

Behind him, Bedivere called 'Farewell!' and the word echoed after Hereward as he ran into the passage.

They fled up the flight of steps. At the top Hereward could see the entrance, already half covered by the dark mass of the rock. His heart pounded and the grinding of rock against rock filled his ears.

By now the way out was little more than a narrow space of daylight. Gwyneth squeezed through it; Hereward hurtled after her, and felt his foot slip on the smooth stone. He stumbled and fell to his hands and knees.

'Help!' he cried, struggling to his feet. 'Don't leave me!'

There was only the thinnest sliver of light left in the passageway. Hereward flung himself forward and felt a strong hand grasp his arm. He was jerked off his feet; the moving stone scraped against his tunic, and then he was standing on the narrow ledge on the hillside, taking in great gulps of air as he tried to stay upright and stop himself from shaking.

Ursus was looking down at him, his blue eyes filled with concern. 'Are you hurt, Hereward?' he asked.

Hereward shook his head and managed to find breath to speak. 'No, I don't think so. Thank you, Ursus.'

'Hereward, I'm sorry!' Gwyneth looked near to tears. 'I thought you were right behind me.'

'I was, but I slipped. It was my own fault.' Turning to Ursus, he asked, 'How did you know that the cavern was there? And how did you know that Bedwyn was Bedivere?'

Ursus smiled, but there was a depth of mystery in his eyes. 'There is more truth in the ancient legends than anyone knows,' he said. 'And every man will find his destiny, if there is someone to show him the path. Go home now,' he went on, 'but tell no one of what you have seen. These men will sleep on until the horn is blown, and the time comes for them to awaken.'

He climbed quickly down the slope and disappeared among the thorn trees. Hereward and Gwyneth watched him go out of sight before turning for home. Hereward's brain was still whirling with the wonder of what he had seen. He could scarcely believe the truth of what they had discovered, or understand the anguish of Bedivere's long years of silence. But his heart lifted at the thought of the sleeping warriors, lying under the Tor until Arthur should call them to defend their country once more.

Gwyneth walked across the inn yard to the archway with her mother's basket tucked under one arm. Four days had passed since they left Bedivere in the heart of the Tor, and already the experience had begun to seem like a dream. Far from being tempted to tell anyone, Gwyneth knew that if she tried everyone would think she was mad.

Few of the villagers had commented on the

disappearance of the man they had known as Bedwyn; no one was surprised that he had not wished to stay in the place where he had been accused of murdering a child.

The fear that had troubled the village was fading quicker than frost in sunlight. The pilgrims were beginning to return, and there were more guests at the Crown. Marion le Fevre was well again thanks to the hermit's herbs and at that very moment was bargaining with Mistress Flax for thread. Life was good, and yet Gwyneth could not stifle a sneaking regret that their adventures were over.

She caught sight of Hereward dashing towards her from the abbey gate on the other side of the street. His face was flushed with excitement. 'Lord Robert Hardwycke is here!' he panted.

'What?' Gwyneth was astonished. She had never expected that Lord Robert would dare to set foot in Glastonbury after what he had done; he could not be sure that Ralph FitzStephen had not made his crime public.

'Edmund too,' Hereward went on. 'They arrived this morning. I just spoke to Brother Padraig. Lord Robert wants to see us. We have to go to the guest lodgings at once.'

Her mother's errands forgotten, Gwyneth eagerly followed her brother across the street. As she hurried through the abbey gateway, she glanced up at the Tor. Secrets enfolded it like mist. Some day, she knew, she would discover more. She and Hereward had not finished with the legends of Glastonbury, nor had their last encounter with the mysterious hermit Ursus.

She spotted Edmund's travelling litter set outside the guest lodgings. Hereward led the way inside, to the same room Lord Robert had occupied before, and tapped on the door.

To Gwyneth's surprise, Lord Ralph Fitz-Stephen's voice summoned them to come in. Suddenly she felt nervous. She half expected to go in and discover the king's steward standing over Lord Robert's body with his sword in his hand.

The room was full of people but at first Gwyneth could only look at one of them. Edmund Hardwycke was directly in front of her, not lying in bed as she had seen him before but sitting in a chair by the fire, with Brother Padraig bending over him. He still looked frail, but his eyes were bright. There was a faint flush in his cheeks and his voice was stronger as he turned his head to greet his friends.

'Hereward, Gwyneth!' he said in delight. 'Good day to you. I didn't expect to see you again so soon.'

'Edmund, you're better!' Hereward exclaimed.

Brother Padraig nodded agreement. 'The improvement is almost miraculous! Truly, God is good.'

'The herbs you sent have done their work,' Lord Robert added from his seat on the other side of the fire. His hair was sleekly brushed, and he had dressed in his finest robes. 'My physician has studied them, and will go on supplying them for Edmund.'

'I'm so glad!' said Gwyneth.

'Edmund will be able to play with me now,' Eleanor FitzStephen chimed in happily. She was sitting in front of the fire with her doll in her arms, the amber necklace around her neck once more; but as she spoke she bounced up and dashed across the room to Lord Ralph. 'Father, Edmund can come and visit us again, can't he?'

Lord Ralph swung her up into his arms. 'Of course, if his father wishes.'

'I do,' said Lord Robert. 'With your leave, we

194

will come again in spring, when the weather improves.'

'By then I might be strong enough to ride,' said Edmund.

Lord Robert looked doubtful, and Brother Padraig said, 'You must not overtax your strength, Edmund.'

The boy laughed. 'I know. But the herbs make me better every day.'

'And we have you to thank,' Lord Robert said, turning to Gwyneth and Hereward. 'For it was you who brought the herbs, and turned me from the foolish course I had chosen.' Glancing at Lord Ralph, he went on, 'My conscience would not let me stay at Hardwycke without trying to make up for the wrong I did. As soon as I saw how your remedies worked on Edmund I knew I had to come back. Lord Ralph has forgiven me, and in penance I have given gold to the abbey to help in the work of rebuilding.'

'For which we thank you,' Brother Padraig said gravely.

'It's little enough, for the life of my son.' To Gwyneth and Hereward he added, 'I have gifts for you, too.' Reaching down beside his chair, he held out something in each hand: for Gwyneth a necklace of blue lapis beads, and for Hereward a handsome leather belt with a silver buckle.

Gwyneth flushed with pleasure as she dropped him a curtsy. 'My lord, there's no need . . .'

'Indeed there is,' said Lord Robert. 'I hope that when you wear them you will think of me as your friend.'

Hereward bowed deeply. 'We will, my lord.'

'It seems we must all thank you for bringing the truth to light yet again.'

The voice was Godfrey de Massard's. In her excitement at seeing Edmund again Gwyneth had not noticed him before, seated in the window alcove out of the circle of firelight. To Gwyneth's surprise he had Eleanor's kitten on his lap, curled up in the folds of his habit.

Gwyneth dropped him a respectful curtsy. 'We only did what we had to, sir, to help Edmund and Bedwyn.'

'Indeed. Then if trouble should strike again, we must call on you.'

Gwyneth had the impression that he was baiting her, and did not know how to reply, but Hereward said stoutly, 'We'll do our best to help, sir—even if the trouble comes from Henry of Truro.'

Father Godfrey's brows shot up; then he relaxed, and Gwyneth caught a glimpse of his smile. 'I should have learned by now not to be surprised by you or your sister, young Hereward,' he admitted. 'And I truly believe you would.'